WINTER WITCHES

AMY PROKOPIS

Amy Prokopis

Cover image by Amy Prokopis

Edited by Lucia Ferrara

Published by Amy Prokopis

First printing edition

www.amyprokopis.com

To my sister

Chapter 1

I COULD FEEL winter before I got to the front of the plane and breathed in the icy air. It was a heavenly forty degrees in Denver and for the briefest of seconds, as I passed from the plane to the jet bridge, I could feel my magic tingling in my veins from the December chill.

Once I was clear of the traffic and had ample space to roll my suitcase behind me, I tugged my phone from my purse and let my fingers fly over the keyboard. I typed out the entire story of the argument I overheard between the cute boy a row ahead of me and his girlfriend and was starting on a second message about the woman across the aisle from me with the cute French bulldog under her seat before I ever thought to ask where she was.

I looked up from my screen and scanned the room of people bundled in puffy coats, some carrying Christmas packages. That's when I spotted her sitting across the walkway with her laptop on her knees and her feet propped up on her suitcase.

"Margot!"

My squeal carried through the room and garnered a lot of attention, but I was too busy running toward my sister and wrapping my arms around her before she could even set her laptop aside.

I let out another squeal and stepped back. Margot was dressed in a pair of blue sweatpants and a gray hoodie with UCLA across the front in yellow. Of course, she was. If Margot was a brand, the store would be full of athleisure and sneakers—and not the cute kind you wear to a college party.

"We are at the airport, you know," Margot said and lifted my purse to look at the champagne-colored leather.

I pulled it from her grasp and rolled my eyes. "You might spend the money Mom and Dad send us when you go to all those bougie team dinners, but I choose to spend all of mine to dress for the future I'd like to have."

I tossed my hair over my shoulder to match the energy and Margot smiled and shook her head.

"I've missed you," she said as she tucked her laptop into her suitcase. "And just so you know, the school pays for those bougie team dinners. It's considered a perk of playing D1."

I held my hands up and feigned innocence as I started toward the moving walkway.

"So, I spend money on clothes. Technically, I can argue that shopping is an educational activity since I am studying fashion. I'm only in my second year at Kent. Let's not talk about our entire childhood of soccer lessons, competitive teams, and that professional player Dad hired."

Margot elbowed me. "You talk like he was David Beckham."

"Who spent all of Daddy's money now?" I teased, the giggle bursting from my lips when Margot's jaw dropped.

"Gross, Madison. Don't ever say that again," she said with pink-tinged cheeks. "And you know that Mom's the breadwinner."

Technically, she was right. Mom's company made more than Dad's, but when they both make more separately than most married people can dream to pool together in a decade... I didn't fully understand the reality of my family's financial state, our entire life really, until I went away to college and realized what the whole "poor college kid" thing looked like. I thought eating Ramen and budgeting meal plans was all a figure of speech.

My roommate was happy to enlighten me and called me out on all my privileged ignorance before I could embarrass myself. Thank God for Rainy.

"I can't believe I am saying it, but I kind of miss them," I said.

Margot groaned. "You miss all the business calls during dinner and them arguing in whispers about who can go on what business trip when? The only one I miss is Marlee."

I shrugged. "I miss her too. When's the last time you talked to her?"

Margot and Marlee always got along better than Marlee and I did. I used to say it was because Marlee insisted on being different, like it was a badge of honor or something, but I know now that it's just because I spent high school caught up in the drama and being seen at the right parties. We were on two different planets, and it took me going to my first college party to realize that everything I'd done in high school was way over-rated. The best part of any party is the people who show up.

"I let her know when your plane would land an hour ago. I call her at least once a week," Margot said and checked her phone.

I stopped just outside the airport entrance, not at all bothered by the cool air. That was one of many nice things about being a winter witch.

"We texted a couple of days ago about Christmas and stuff," I said. I didn't want to do the math on my current relationship with Marlee, because I was sure it was severely lacking compared to Margot's schedule. Even with all the practicing and weightlifting sessions, she managed to call our little sister once a week.

Margot didn't reply, she was too busy looking at her phone. The silver SUV caught my attention as it pulled to the curb a few feet away. I walked ahead of Margot to put my suitcase in the trunk. Mom always kept her car spotless, so I was surprised when the trunk opened to reveal a backpack, a box of old books, and a throw blanket that looked like someone had just tossed it in.

Marlee.

I sat my suitcase next to the box and Margot slid hers in next to mine. I caught Marlee's gaze in the rearview mirror before Margot pressed the button to close the trunk door.

"Shotgun!" Margot called, already climbing into the seat when I rounded the back of the SUV.

"I thought Mom and Dad were coming," I said as I settled into the backseat.

Marlee looked over her shoulder at me. "They were both stuck in Zoom calls when I left."

"Both of them?" I asked.

Marlee nodded. Her expression was every bit as annoyed as I felt.

"So, what's new?" Margot asked, her comment not really directed at anyone.

"My final exam results should be posted this week," I answered as we pulled away from the curb and joined the line of cars eager to exit. "My professor liked my designs so much that I think I'm going to try making them in my sewing class next semester."

Margot nodded in the front seat, and I wasn't sure if it was in response to me or the Taylor Swift song that just started drifting through the car.

"So, you're not in a relationship? Not even talking to anyone?" Marlee asked, sounding bored with the conversation as she passed through the toll booth for the airport and started toward the highway.

Margot laughed.

I groaned. "Is it so hard to believe that maybe I am actively choosing not to get into a relationship with someone?"

"When was the last time you were single?" Margot said between her laughter.

Marlee smirked from the driver's seat but didn't say a word. Good thing too, because I was prepared to point out how little she knew about boys and dating.

"I know. I was always so boy-crazy in high school and dated just about anyone who showed interest, but that's so dumb to me now. I haven't even thought about going on a date since freshman year and I don't plan on starting now. I am happy taking my classes and planning my business," I said and felt the irritation melt away as the words came out.

"What is the business plan anyway?" Marlee asked. Always the cynical one.

"Making clothes, right? Don't you want to own a brand?" Margot asked and turned in the front seat to look at me.

She wasn't wrong, not exactly anyway. I wanted to be my own brand and run the whole business, but after everything I learned from my first year of college and the research I'd been doing into the fashion industry, I decided that high fashion, as amazing and interesting as it was, is overrated. All it took was looking into the actual costs of creating products for me to realize that the price tag didn't match the product most of the time. It's all hype. You, me, and the entire planet Earth are paying for the hype surrounding those expensive brand names and that's pretty much it.

Do you know what is much cooler than being sought after? Being a household name. We all may dream of owning a Supreme sweatshirt, but everyone knows the comfort of a Gildan pullover. The tried and true. It's your high-school cheer team's warmup sweatshirt and you will never give it away because it's that comfortable and looks just as good as any other hoodie with a little writing across the front.

Buy good quality materials. Create cute designs. Don't upcharge for the brand name. Sell millions and millions. That's what I dream of. Not only does that sound just as good as being some fancy brand name, but I know I can do it and do it well.

"That's the idea," I said. It wasn't exactly the picture my family had in mind for me, but oh well. Eventually, they'd find out about my website anyway. There aren't any products there yet. Mostly I was trying out my hand at web design, so I wouldn't have to learn it all while trying to sell clothes. That's where Rainy came in. When I was in high school, I wouldn't have dreamed of spending my free time talking about HTML code and everything else Rainy was trying to teach me, but now I was thankful for my IT-majoring bestie.

Marlee snorted and I saw her roll her eyes. "Figures."

"What are you going to do, run a bookstore?" I asked, not able to contain myself.

Margot spoke before Marlee got a chance. "She's Heritage City Academy's valedictorian. She had already been accepted to Yale. She's going to study political science and go to law school."

"English," Marlee corrected and then added, "then law school," in a much softer voice.

How did I not know that she got accepted to Yale?

"You didn't tell me about getting into Yale," I yelled over the radio.

Marlee looked more uncomfortable than usual.

"I was still deciding," Marlee defended.

Of course, she got into more than one Ivy.

"I'm surprised you haven't changed your major to neuro-surgery," Marlee said. "Every time you respond to either of us your eyes roll back so far, I'm sure you can see your brain. At this rate, you'll be an expert by noon."

Margot burst into laughter so loud and consuming that it drowned out the entire chorus of "Bejeweled." I reached over the back of her seat and tugged her ponytail until she turned around to look at me.

"You have to admit that it was a good burn," she said, wiping at the tears in her eyes.

I resisted the urge to roll my eyes this time. "Yes, we all know that Marlee Sinclair is going to graduate *summa cum laude* at Yale and inherit both our parents' companies. I didn't need the joke to realize that fact."

It was Marlee's turn to roll her eyes.

I was nice and didn't point out the gesture.

Chapter 2

MARLEE WAS A SUPER CAUTIOUS DRIVER, which normally annoyed me. Today, it allowed me the time to watch the snow swirling over the pavement and unwind with my magic. Winter witches had power year-round, sure, but it was practically useless compared to the power surge we got after the first snowfall of the season.

There were witches for every season. Summer witches had fire powers, which was great when we all sat outside and roasted marshmallows at events. Spring witches could control the earth. They make great farmers. Fall witches had control of the air. I've never met one because they mostly live in windy places or areas where the weather is dramatic, like Tornado Alley. Dad always called them the "four covens" even though covens aren't really a thing in the witch world the way most people would imagine. But it's the closest explanation for what it feels like when you get a bunch of winter witches together, though and that's sort of why places like Crescent Peak exist.

Crescent Peak isn't that far from Heritage City. Most people would just drive from Heritage City to Crescent Peak to enjoy the adorable tourist town, but not my family. It was a family tradition to spend the winter holiday in Crescent Peak in the cabin, which Rainy told me was better described as a mountain mansion.

Mom always talked like it was a matter of practicality to move up there each winter seeing as the cabin stayed decorated for Christmas year-round. Unlike Heritage City, Crescent Peak was a witch haven. It was full of winter witches most of the year, but it was a hotspot for us during the winter when our powers were at their strongest.

Marlee turned onto the long stretch of pavement that led to our family home and I felt... strange. Yeah, I grew up with the gigantic front lawn and the pond, but I couldn't help but notice all the smaller details now like the pristine condition of the boathouse. I knew now that it only looked so neat because of the staff my family hired to keep it that way. Also, who in the landlocked state had a pond on their property big enough for a boathouse? They were small boats, but still...

"If Mom and Dad are still tied up in business things, then I want to go ice skating," Margot said. I wanted to ask if her coach allowed her to do that over Christmas break, but I knew her better than to question her judgment. Where soccer was involved, Margot was serious.

Marlee pulled into the garage next to Dad's Jeep and put the SUV in park before she answered. "That's where everyone in Heritage City will be."

She said it like it was a bad thing, but I knew it just meant that she wanted some alone time. For every hour of social time you got out of Marlee, you could guarantee she'd go missing for two. Mom always said she was just introverted. I call her anti-social.

"What book are you reading?" I asked as we all got out of the car and went to the trunk.

Marlee paused like she was going to launch into an argument, but let out a sigh instead and said, "My school lit club is reading *Wuthering Heights* over break, and I just got to the part where Cathy dies."

I feigned a gasp. "A spoiler warning would've been nice."

I wrapped my arms around Marlee and swore I was teasing, even though I had no idea what *Wuthering Heights* was about and I had no any plans to ever suffer through it. Margot and I grabbed our suitcases and rolled them into the house.

Our rooms were upstairs and down a wing to the right. No lie, we all knew Mom and Dad would be busy with something work-related, so it wasn't a surprise to see Mom on the phone in the kitchen and Dad talking to his laptop screen in the living room as we made our way upstairs.

At the end of the hall was a communal space with a TV mounted on the far wall and several theater-style chairs where Margot and I agreed to meet once we were both ready to go skating. Once *I* was ready to go skating.

My bedroom was exactly as I remembered it. The walls were bubblegum pink with an accent wall of big white polka dots behind the bed. My collage of photos from high school was still there above my vanity mirror and my bathroom to the left still smelled like the floral plug-in I loved before Rainy introduced me to those wooden-wick candles during freshman year.

It took me much longer than normal to unpack. I found myself looking at all the photos above my dresser of old friends I hadn't talked to since graduation and cheer competitions I no longer remembered. I laid out an outfit for myself that I knew would be comfortable to ice skate in, but also look good for Instagram photos. Once everything was put away neatly in their drawers, I donned the lavender-colored leggings and matching top. My white jacket would look great and keep me warm on the ice.

I knew that Margot was waiting for me by now, but I took the time to twist my hair into two braids over my shoulders anyway and add a little shimmery eyeshadow to the corners of my eyes. Sparkly like snow on Christmas.

Margot had barely changed at all. The only difference was the pair of leggings she wore instead of the sweatpants she had on at the airport. I could now see the effects of all the training she'd been doing at UCLA. She was still lean the way she'd always been, but now her calves were rounder, and her thighs were shaped like those Gymshark girls all over Instagram.

"Ready?" I asked.

Margot gave me that look like she wanted to tell me just how long she'd been ready to go, but she just stood up instead.

"Should we ask Marlee again? You know, just to be sure?" I asked.

Margot shook her head and led the way down the hall. "I already did. She's busy with her book."

When we got downstairs, Dad was packing up his laptop. He smiled up at us.

"I'm doing ribs for dinner," he announced, rubbing his hands together.

"Sounds great," I told him.

His eyes went to the purse at my hip, back to my face, and then to Margot's.

"Leaving already?" he asked.

"We wanted to go skating before we head up to the cabin tomorrow," Margot answered as Mom appeared in the kitchen doorway, still on the phone. She waved at both of us and then mouthed the words *have fun* before walking back into the kitchen.

"Be back by seven for the ribs. You won't want to miss it," Dad said and then pointed at Margot with a smile on his face. "You need that protein, am I right, Superstar?"

She giggled and said, "Back by seven."

I didn't give her a chance to ask which car we were taking when we reached the mudroom. I took the keys to my bubblegum-pink Jeep from the hook on the wall and went straight out the door.

"I hope I don't run into people from high school," I said and climbed into the driver's seat.

Margot snorted as she got in. "Well, if we do they will all see you first. Kind of hard to miss a pink car."

Everyone in our family owned a Jeep. Not so much because we all liked Jeeps. Mostly, because Dad liked them, and it was one of the few cars where wild colors didn't look strange. You didn't see many pink SUVs on the highway. A pink Jeep though? That's adorable. Mine was parked between Margot's electric-blue Jeep and Marlee's orange Jeep.

It had stopped snowing, leaving a dusting of white over the front lawn. I couldn't wait to get into the mountains tomorrow where everything would be covered in a white blanket.

Margot tuned the radio to a pop station while I did a two-point turn and started back down the long driveway. I missed my Jeep. Back in Kent, I didn't have a car. Mom and Dad told me I could go buy one, but after the first month of walking campus, learning how public transportation worked, and becoming good friends with Rainy I forgot about it. Rainy had a Toyota Corolla that she would let me drive sometimes if I needed to, so I was a little out of practice when it came to the heated seats and touchscreen controls of the Jeep.

"The bakery is a pot dispensary now?" I asked as we rounded the bend toward town.

Margot looked up from her phone and muttered, "Apparently."

"What are you looking at? Is that TikTok?" I asked, glancing at the video playing on her screen. I gasped when I saw the soccer ball fly past the screen. "Don't tell me you're studying film. You're not even in season yet!"

"Coach says I play well, but I should watch some games to sharpen my senses and know what to look for." Margot closed the video and stuck her phone in her pocket. "No more soccer. I swear."

I knew that was a big, fat lie. She'd probably be out in the snow running drills like she used to every Christmas at the cabin. I was too distracted to comment though. The skating rink was packed with people. I parked in the first free spot I found. Most of the people were here for the burger place just next door, but there were still at least a dozen skating circles on the ice.

"Shoot," Margot said as she joined me at the back of the Jeep. "We should've brought our skates from home. I didn't think about the fact that we'd be borrowing some here."

Ugh. I hadn't either. Ice skating was something we'd both grown up doing, so much so that when we were little Margot said she was going to be a professional soccer player and go to the Olympics for figure skating on the side. I took figure skating lessons a few years in Denver while Margot was at soccer practice. Marlee would go skating with us, but it wasn't really her thing. The Sinclair athletic gene skipped our little sister.

We paid for our shoes and found a bench. Margot gathered our things and took them to the locker station while I made my way toward the entrance to the rink. I stopped short of stepping on the ice when I heard a familiar laugh from a group of girls as they skated by.

Winnie Maxwell looked the same as the last time I saw her. Her thick brown hair hung in loose curls down her back. Her skin was flawless, and she looked in better shape than I remember her ever being in high school. The only thing that wasn't gorgeous about her was the way she laughed. That laugh was enough to send me right back to freshman year of high school and made me irritated all over again. It sounded like a squeaky toy, a high-pitched giggle that I was still to this day convinced was a conscious effort just to appear all cute and innocent to boys.

Winnie and her two friends, girls I didn't recognize, rounded the corner of the rink and I got a look at them as they skated in a straight line. They were all wearing different oversized sweatshirts, but the same Greek letters were there across all three of their chests. They were sorority sisters and to make matters worse, they were in the same sorority as I was. Ugh.

"Is that Winnie Maxwell?" Margot asked.

I glanced at her, wondering how long she'd been standing there.

"Yes," I said, the word coming out like the hiss of a tea kettle.

"What does she do now?"

"I don't know, and I don't really care. She's the last person I hoped to ever run into for the rest of my life."

Margot elbowed me. "Ignore her and let's just have a good time."

I followed her onto the ice and we started skating around the rink. It didn't take us many laps to fall back in time to when we were little. I found myself remembering different moves I'd learned from my lessons; muscle memory was the only explanation for the basic turns I didn't know I could do anymore. I had forgotten about Winnie and her entourage until the moment Margot and I made our way to the exit, and she nearly sent me face-first onto the ice.

"I'm sorry," Winnie said before doing a double take. "Madison Sinclair? I thought you looked familiar. How have you been?"

There was no way she didn't recognize me the first time. We'd gone to school together forever, we were even good friends through elementary school before things got competitive. We were cheerleaders together, on all the school social clubs together, not to mention connected outside of school since her family were also winter witches. Even during school

breaks, I couldn't escape her thanks to all our witchy cele-
brations.

"Great. I go to school out of state," I told her, not bothering
to ask how she was as I inched my way toward the exit. I moved
from the ice to the rubber mat before she could make further
conversation.

"We'll have to catch up later," she called out, her friendly
smile fading the minute she turned back to her sorority sisters
and began whispering.

I faced Margot, who offered a sympathetic smile.

"Well, at least you're not less successful than she is," she said.

"Even," I groaned and passed her for our bench.

Even was the story of my life when it came to the petty
competition between Winnie Maxwell and me. I don't know
what changed between elementary and middle school except
that we were suddenly involved in all the same things and
always dead even when it came to who had what position.
Senior year, our cheer coach broke her own rules to declare us
co-captains. We were both in the running for homecoming
queen, but I came down with the flu the week of the dance and
had to give up my spot on the court. Winnie won the crown and
insisted ever since that it made her better. It was so petty. I
knew it then and I know it now, but that didn't make the mean-
girl feud any less antagonistic.

"I know it's annoying, but maybe we won't see her as much
as you think in Crescent Peak," Margot said.

I hoped she was right. Even though I knew I had played the
game back in high school the same way that Winnie had, I
wanted to just forget about it and move forward. I had my
degree to focus on. I had my website. I was better off thinking
about the things that actually mattered right now rather than
some stupid battle I'd waged back in high school.

We exchanged our skates for our shoes and I noticed the line
that had formed at the booth. There were several groups of

eager skaters waiting to pay for their skates. It would take us forever to turn in our skates and locker keys.

"What if you stand in line to turn in our skates and I go get us hot chocolates?" I asked, pouting my lip at my sister in hopes it would convince her.

Margot let out a sigh and took my skates. I went in the opposite direction toward the food truck. A man with a thick, red beard appeared in the window to take my order. Once I paid, I stood off to the side and watched the skaters on the rink.

There was a young couple holding hands as they struggled to find their balance. The adorable display was their first mistake. Both of them fell to the ice when the man lost his footing. The blonde girl fell onto his chest, both laughing hysterically once they recovered. The blonde had just pressed her lips against his when my name was called at the window.

"Careful," the red-bearded man said. "We just made a new batch, so it's pretty hot. Maybe let it cool off for a bit before you drink it."

"Thanks," I told him and lifted the Styrofoam cups from the window ledge.

My stomach sank when I saw Winnie heading my way, smiling like running into me had been the best part of her day. Her mouth formed an O of amazement and she gestured from my purse to hers.

"Oh my god, we are twinning," she said and turned to the truck window to order her hot chocolate. She glanced at the cups in my hands before looking back at the barista to tell him she wanted hers without the whipped cream and sprinkles. "I don't want to gain any holiday weight."

I knew my face would betray me, so I turned to the table on my right and sat the cups down. I took two lids from a stack and pressed them on top, whipped cream coming out the hole on top. I licked the top of my lid as Winnie appeared next to me with her boring cup of cocoa.

"So, what do you do now? I study business in Denver. I'm involved in the leadership committee of my sorority. I'm a part of a Future Female Leaders of America club on campus. What do *you* do?"

She listed everything off so casually but finished with a challenging tone.

"I am also super involved with my sorority, and I study fashion design. I go to Kent State University. It's one of the best universities for fashion in the states." I tried imitating her air of nonchalance but had a hard time containing my satisfaction.

Winnie took a couple of napkins from the table and then turned to face me. "Are you seeing anyone?"

"No. I'm just so focused on my major."

"Yeah. I get that. Some people just can't balance school and social life and that's fine. Not everyone meets their person in college."

Ugh. Maybe she'd burn her tongue on the hot chocolate like the man warned me about.

"Are you seeing anyone?" I asked, fighting the urge to respond to her last jab. I could see from the twitch of her lips that something had happened.

"I actually just got out of a relationship." She said the words slowly like she regretted telling me.

"I'm sorry. Getting broken up with sucks," I said and took a sip of my drink, enduring the scalding liquid just out of spite.

"Oh no," Winnie said and let out a snort. "I broke up with him."

"Why?" I asked.

She paused. She didn't expect me to ask for the details.

"He was hot, like *super* hot, but he just wasn't as involved as I am, and he didn't like to go out to all the events… Things just didn't click." She shrugged like she didn't care, but the apathy didn't reach her eyes. This was a fresh wound.

"So, you dump your boring boyfriend and go home for the

holidays… What's your plan for Crescent Peak this year?" Part of the season involved a winter celebration, which included a gala with all the glamor and drama of a Hollywood party. Everyone came dressed in white to match the snow and after our yearly ritual, the party began, and we danced into the morning hours.

"I think I'm going to do the single thing and enjoy the dance with my girls," Winnie said as she pressed a lid on her cup. "But you know how that goes. Boys just seem to appear and sometimes, I indulge them." She let out one of those annoying giggles. That's always how Winnie got into relationships though. She'd just bounce around school, being Winnie, and the boys would come to her until one was always around her, and then… Relationship. I wondered if Boring Boyfriend had done the same thing. He probably had.

"Well, you know what they say about indulging," I said and held up my cup for reference. "A little sugar every now and then is a treat, but too much too often and you'll rot your teeth."

Winnie's expression fell and the satisfaction I felt only blossomed. I really shouldn't have said it. I should've let the nasty thought float past and saved it for later when I'd fantasize about owning this interaction later, but I couldn't resist.

Winnie grabbed my wrist before I could turn from her, a sweet smile back on her face. "No matter how much time passes, some things just never change. For instance, you can't spell Winnie without W-I-N."

She smirked and went back to her friends who were sitting on a bench talking. She was right about some things never changing. Winnie always had to have the last word and when I raised my lips to my cup and felt how cold the lid was, I knew she had to be laughing inside as she walked away.

I pulled off the lid and just as I thought, the hot chocolate inside was frozen solid.

Chapter 3

I REPACKED my suitcase with a new set of winter outfits and was the last person in my family to get to the living room. I was dressed down, at least by my standards, and I was still more dressed up than anyone else in my jeans, heeled boots, and white sweater.

"We need to make a couple of stops on the way up," Mom said, keys jingling as she took them out of her purse.

I glanced at my sisters. Marlee had *Wuthering Heights* tucked under one arm, her bookmark sandwiched between the pages centimeters from the back cover. Margot adjusted her ponytail; Dad wrapped an arm around her shoulders.

"We could use some help," he said. "I'll need a hand when we pick up firewood."

Eager to avoid that excursion, I volunteered myself for a task. "I'll drive up to the cabin and turn everything on."

"That's a good idea," Margot said. "You can take Marlee."

I was sure my annoyance was obvious. Maybe she was just used to it, but Marlee didn't say a word.

"The SUV will be pretty packed after we pick everything up. It'll be more comfortable that way," Mom said and started for the garage.

I didn't argue, but I did stick my tongue out at Margot when

Marlee wasn't looking. Mom, Dad, and Margot left ahead of us. Marlee loaded our suitcases into the back of my Jeep while I mentally prepared for the boring drive up the mountain.

"Any music requests?" I asked as Marlee climbed into the Jeep.

She shrugged and sank into her seat. "You pick." She opened her book to the bookmarked page. "I want to finish this book so I can write my essay over it."

"Wow," I said and cued up the newest Taylor Swift album. "Most seniors are over the high school thing by this point in the year."

Marlee didn't reply, so I turned my attention to the music and backed out of the garage. Crescent Peak was about a forty-five-minute drive, most of it on a two-lane road that wound through the trees up a mountain not far outside of Heritage City.

"They finished the gym? That was fast," I commented as we passed the outskirts of town where Heritage City Academy was. The gym had the school mascot, an elk, on the side of the building that faced the highway.

"They wanted to have it finished for volleyball season," Marlee said and turned the page of her book. I hadn't expected to get a comment at all from her and it was probably the last one I would get for the whole trip based on how seriously she stared down at the pages of *Wuthering Heights*.

It snowed overnight, the road the only stretch of ground not coated in a layer of white. I focused on the lyrics of the song, resisting the urge to sing along as we started our climb up the mountain. It was beautiful and I realized now that I hadn't spent any time outdoors since I got here. That was unacceptable. Unheard of for a winter witch to stay inside by the fire.

I remembered the mercantile when I saw the small wooden sign a few miles out. McAdams Mercantile sold all kinds of things, but they were best known for the Christmas tree farm behind the big red barn. Inside the barn, they sold handmade goods and farm-grown foods, and had a small section for branded clothing. The McAdams were one of the few non-witch families that stayed in Crescent Peak. I didn't know any of them personally— us witches all stuck together in Crescent Peak— but I could point out the members of the family if I had to.

I pulled onto the stretch of gravel road at the sign, able to see the huge barn a few yards away. Their parking lot was mostly empty, just a few work trucks parked over the snow.

"We're stopping?" Marlee asked, looking up from her book.

"I just wanted to shop around before we went up to the cabin, you know?" I said. Marlee's expression said it all. She did not know, and she wouldn't be joining me.

I parked next to a silver truck. "I'll be just a moment."

"I'm on the last chapter, so I'll be here," Marlee said in a sing-song tone without looking up from the page.

I brought my purse even though I didn't plan on buying anything. What I really wanted to do was walk between the trees behind the barn, especially with so few people here to witness. The magic was buzzing so intensely in my veins that I walked a little faster toward the barn.

An elderly couple were the only people walking the aisles inside. Mrs. McAdams and a man I didn't recognize worked behind the register in the corner. They were too busy unpacking green bars of soap into a display basket to notice me as I went for the open barn door at the back.

The trees were all at least seven feet tall, some taller. They were in neat rows that went on forever. Wooden poles strung lights across the field that made for a romantic nighttime atmosphere.

Every year, my family would come to the mercantile the first night we were in the cabin to pick a tree. There was nothing like the smell of fresh evergreen in your living room. We always had four. Two for the front living room and two for the back. We usually split our efforts to decorate all four, with Mom and Dad finding some kind of work to do and leaving Margot, Marlee, and me to decorate the fourth tree last minute. Decorating was one of my favorite things to do and since our cabin stayed decorated for Christmas all year, the tree was the only opportunity I got.

I walked past the first row of trees and kept going, glad that the snow was pretty compact, so my heels didn't sink too far. It felt like the magic would burst from my fingertips, but I wouldn't let it until I was sure no one could see me from the barn. I walked for several minutes, putting the barn several yards away.

I let out a deep breath and I felt everything melt away and the magic flowed easily. Snow fluttered around me like I was in my own snow globe. I held my right hand up and focused on my palm until snow gathered there and formed a tight ball, then another, and then a third to complete the snowman.

I felt warm; it was something only winter witches would understand. When I used my powers or allowed them to just be and not worry about reining them deep inside, it felt like I was under a cashmere blanket. The season didn't chill us the way it did most people. It is when we feel the most comfortable and our powers are at their greatest.

"Whoa! What the…"

I tensed. I pushed every ounce of witchy power deep down, but I knew it didn't matter. He had dark hair that poked out from the gray beanie and wore a pullover with the McAdams Mercantile logo on the front. He was huge. Well, not *huge* the way Dwayne Johnson is, but like six-three at least and muscular enough to suggest he was the staff member responsible for chopping down and carrying the seven-foot trees across the field.

He looked back at me in complete shock. Like, his jaw

dropped he was so shocked. It would've been a little funny except that as he recovered, he gave me a once-over the way many a frat boy did before I rejected their advances.

"What do you want?" I asked.

His thick brow furrowed. "What? What do you mean?"

I groaned. "In return for not telling anyone what you saw."

Six-foot-three lumberjack just stared back at me more confused. "Oh. Yeah. What was all of that? Are you some kind of magician?"

I ignored the question and turned on my heel, walking toward the end of the row quickly.

"Wait! Wait," he called out. I could hear the crunch of snow under his feet. He came around me, stopping me in my tracks. "You're a witch."

"Are you saying that because I didn't compliment your big muscles or…" I let the truth hang in the air for him to vocalize or not. Hopefully not. I wasn't that lucky though.

"I mean a real one, like a witch with magical powers," he said while wiggling his fingers. "I didn't mean to stare, but I was looking for a wire. That didn't explain all the snow though. I know you don't have a snowblower up your shirt or anything. That's stupid, I can't believe I even said that aloud."

My heart was racing in my chest now. This was just great. It wasn't like non-magical people didn't know about us. Some did, but it wasn't because we mentioned it as our party trick when we went to happy hour. Sometimes, we fell in love and shared our secrets with our partners. Sometimes, we told our best friends. Sometimes, though rarely and at a huge cost to our safety, people found out.

We might have to leave Crescent Peak and sell the cabin. Heritage City wasn't that far away. Would my parents have to move from there too? Would it put the rest of the witches in Crescent Peak at risk? We weren't in witch-burning times anymore, but it didn't mean we couldn't become outcasts or lose our jobs. Weirdo religious types liked to seek us out and terrorize us. Maybe everyone would think this guy was crazy. Was that possible?

I laughed and hoped it didn't sound fake. "Do you hear yourself right now?"

"I know what I saw," he said before I could take more than one step to pass him.

"What? What did you see?" I asked and turned to him. I put crossed my arms and put on my best resting bitch face. If calling him crazy didn't work, maybe intimidating would. "You saw… me holding some snow? Kicking snow into the air? Making it all flutter around me?"

He shook his head, a serious expression on his face. "Magic."

"Magic?" I asked, my voice softer than I intended.

He nodded and smirked. "I should tell the nearest magistrate." He smirked.

"Oh my God." I walked past him, bouncing off him when I tried to bump his shoulder with mine. I continued toward the end of the row.

"I'm going to tell the town to gather wood," he said, following me. "Got to get a pyre ready."

"Not funny." I focused on the last tree just a yard away.

"Hey, everyone!" He yelled loud enough that his voice echoed over the field and made my heart stop dead in my chest. "Get your pitchforks ready!"

I turned around the pushed his chest hard, but he didn't even take a step back.

He smiled back at me. "Easy, ice queen."

"What do you want?"

"For?"

I pressed my right foot deeper into the snow. "What will keep you from telling anyone about this?"

His expression fell. It was like he hadn't even considered it. It made me feel a little better. He didn't seem the type to ask for anything creepy. That was my worst nightmare after some of the frat boy interactions I had freshman year. It was one of many reasons I was done with the whole wild party, popularity contest I used to dream of in high school.

"I swear I won't tell anyone."

I snorted. "You think I'll just believe you? No, seriously. What do you really want?"

He looked offended. "Ouch. I swear I'm a man of my word, Elsa."

The joke was so on the nose that I actually felt my eyes roll. He extended his gloved hand, pinky up.

"What do you want?" I asked, not moving.

After a moment, he dropped his hand and straightened up. He looked like he was thinking hard about what to say next. A little hill rose between his brows.

"Come back here tomorrow before noon and I'll tell you," he finally said and started to back away. "Ask for Jared."

"Geez," I said as he walked away, one step for him the same as two for me. I wanted to scream. I thought about freezing him like a popsicle for a moment but decided it would just make things worse. It wasn't like I had any plans. Mom and Dad would work like usual. We might have family dinners if they could wrap up whatever business they had by then. Marlee would keep to herself. Margot would probably practice most of the day. I was a little surprised that she came home this year at all with how worried she was about securing her starting position.

I walked back to the barn, keeping several yards behind Jared. He went behind the counter when we got to the barn and kissed the woman on the cheek as he pulled off his work gloves. So, he was a McAdams. I could feel his eyes on me as I left the barn and went back to the Jeep.

"What took you so long?" Marlee asked, looking up from her phone.

Wuthering Heights was sitting on the dash with the bookmark between the cover and the front page. I noticed the door of the silver truck open to her right. Jared McAdams met my gaze and gave me a nod of acknowledgment before starting the truck and backing up.

"Nothing," I said and started the Jeep.

Chapter 4

MARLEE VANISHED, probably to her bedroom, before I had finished turning everything on in the cabin. I checked to make sure the electricity was on and that the water worked. Mom, Dad, and Margot came in as I started to assess the kitchen.

"Anyone want hot chocolate?" I asked.

"I'm on a dairy-free and sugar-free diet," Mom said as she pulled her phone from her pocket and dropped her keys and purse on the counter next to me.

Dad pressed his lips to my temple. "I'm going to check some emails. I have to contact the investors before holiday hours take effect."

"I'll have some," Margot said and hopped onto a barstool opposite me.

I started to unpack the groceries they'd brought in, leaving out the ingredients I needed.

"You gather firewood?" I asked.

"Yup."

"Any splinters?"

She smiled at my joke and held up her hands as if to prove she was unscathed.

"How was the trip here with Marlee?"

I paused as I moved the veggies into the fridge for a moment.

Marlee and I had barely spoken more than a few words. It wasn't that I was trying to ignore her. I loved my sister, but I just couldn't relate to her. I don't understand her and that's fine, but it means that I don't really know her. What would happen once we were all in our careers and living in different cities?

"Good," I answered as I finished unpacking. "She went to read her book."

Margot nodded. I poured water into the tea kettle and started to warm it over the stove.

"I'm going to use the gym downstairs tomorrow morning. Want to join?"

I moved two mugs, both in the shape of snowmen, from the cabinet to the counter.

"I would, but I'm going out tomorrow morning." I could see the curiosity on her face and was glad that the kettle chose that moment to start whistling. I moved it from the heat and poured the hot water into the mugs, mixing the ingredients in. Margot leaned over the counter for the whipped cream, forming a perfect swirl over the liquid.

"How about we meet up for lunch tomorrow?" Margot asked, wiping the whipped cream off her nose after taking a sip.

I paused with the can of whipped cream in one hand, Winnie's voice in the back of my head. I put the cap back on the can and set it aside. "Sounds fun. We could meet at the diner in town."

"I'll bring Marlee and you can meet us there after your morning thing."

I was glad she didn't ask me any questions. In Crescent Peak though, I could be meeting up with several different witches or warlocks. That's how I usually made it through the holidays, keeping busy to avoid Mom and Dad's arguments about whose work was more important.

Margot and I talked about college while we drank our hot chocolate until Dad reappeared at seven to make dinner.

Cooking was the only non-work thing he ever did. He loved it and he was really good at it. He asked Margot all about her soccer training as he worked over the stove. I stuck around until I lost track of what they were talking about.

My bedroom in the cabin was like the one back home—pink. Rope lights outlined the baseboards and crown molding and cast a soft light over the room. I started to hang up my clothes in the closet, stopping when I noticed a family photo that had been taken at the mercantile. I picked the frame up from the dresser to look closer at the people in the background walking the rows of trees under the lights.

There he was, standing next to a tree with a chainsaw. Jared McAdams. If I had only known who he was then… What? I wasn't sure where the thought was meant to go. Back then, I wouldn't have noticed him anyway. I was too concerned with making sure I looked better at the Winter Solstice Gala than Winnie.

I had just hung up the dress I made for this year's gala. I was so proud of the white ballgown. Not only was it gorgeous, but I made it myself and got the highest grade in my textiles class for the project. No one in the world owned this gown; it was unique. I couldn't wait to wear it. Just thinking about it made me feel beautiful, and that's all that mattered.

But looking better than Winnie Maxwell would be a bonus.

"Dad said dinner is ready," Marlee said from my doorway.

"Tell them I'm just finishing unpacking. I'll catch up."

"We aren't eating together anyway," Marlee said. "Mom's still on her call and Dad said if she wasn't going to eat with us, then we were going to eat while she sends her emails."

I let out a sigh. Figures.

"I'll be down in a minute."

That was one thing I really admired about Marlee. Whenever someone responded to her with a tone or took something out on her, she turned the other cheek. She didn't take anything personally. As Mom said, Marlee marched to the beat of her own drum. If I had spent my senior year with the same attitude, she had toward hers, things would've been a lot easier.

I THOUGHT ABOUT DRESSING DOWN, like way down, as I got ready for the morning at the mercantile. I had to think about yesterday's interaction with Jared to be convinced that he wouldn't make it creepy today. He had me all alone. He could've done something then if he really wanted to. It was fine. Just me doing whatever to make sure he didn't blab to the entire mountain that I'm a witch. Totally fine.

I curled the ends of my hair so it would look less boring peeking out under my pink beanie. I wore a pale pink sweatshirt with the word *babe* embroidered in pink over my left breast. I pulled on a pair of jeans and decided to pull on my flat boots just in case whatever he had planned was outdoorsy. Also, just in case I had to run.

It's fine. I kept reminding myself that as I did my makeup.

I noticed that I matched the Jeep too perfectly as I went to defrost the windshield, so I took a couple of photos for Instagram while I waited. Once the windshield was clear, I started back down the mountain toward the mercantile. I sat with the engine off for a moment in the parking lot. Was this a good idea? Maybe I was giving this guy too much credit when I decided he wasn't planning something creepy.

I opened Instagram and started to draft my post, attaching the photo of me lounging in the front seat of the Jeep with the door open. I had to put the camera on timer and prop it up in a tree to get the shot, but all it took was a single filter to make the fake-candid shot look moody. I typed out the caption *Snow Bunny or Snow Hunny?*

I posted the photo and then looked up at the barn. There

were a few more cars here than yesterday. That was a good sign. I felt a little better watching the families mill about inside the barn. I took a deep breath, gathered my purse, and stepped out of the Jeep.

I followed a family with three small kids who struggled to walk in the snow to the barn. Mrs. McAdams and the same man from yesterday were working inside the barn, Mrs. McAdams putting together the soap display using the baskets she had created yesterday while the man hung up their branded sweat-shirts on the left wall. I chose him as my target.

"You guys should add other graphic tees to your stock," I said, gaining his attention.

"What did you have in mind?" he asked and turned from the wall.

I pointed to my sweatshirt. "You can charge forty or so for something like this just because it's embroidered. It's a simple design, but the sweatshirt is quality, and it actually keeps you warm, unlike most of those fancy graphic tees that go for a complicated design and cheap materials."

He looked impressed. "I might ask you more about all that later if you have the time."

"I'll be around," I said and looked over the shop for the dark-haired boy. "I'm here for Jared."

He was surprised but looked over the shop like I had, only he found who he was looking for in Mrs. McAdams.

"Jo," he called. The dark-haired woman looked up. "Where's Jared?"

She glanced at me, looking me over the way Jared had, and then looked back at the man.

"He's processing the old trees in the shop like he usually does at nine," she said, her tone a little irritated. "Why?"

Surely, she knew why. She saw me standing there. She had to know I'd asked. She just didn't want to speak to me directly. Classic girl move.

"Um, well…" the man stammered, looking from me to Mrs. McAdams and then back at me again. "What's your name?"

"Madison Sinclair."

He looked back at Mrs. McAdams again and said, "Madison is looking for him."

"I see that, Mark. I just…" Mrs. McAdams let out a sigh and came around the register, stopping in the middle of the walkway when a woman approached the register with a full basket to check out.

"I'll show her the way," Mark said.

Mrs. McAdams nodded her head, gave me another once-over, and then went back to her post.

"So, Mark," I started as we went through the back door of the barn. Instead of leading me to the row of trees, we took a right toward a workshop between the barn and the main house. "Are you a McAdams too?"

"Yup," he said. "Joanne and I are siblings. Our parents owned this farm and then our grandparents and so on. How do you know Jared?"

How to explain it…

"My family has a cabin in Crescent Peak," I said and hoped that was enough. Thankfully, Mark didn't ask any more questions before he opened the shop door.

"This young lady was looking for you," Mark said. Something about the way he said it carrying a warning.

Jared looked up from the wooden table. He sat aside a piece of evergreen and came around the table.

"Thanks," I told Mark.

"Tell my mom that I'm about finished and then I'll walk the rows," Jared said.

Mark nodded and went back outside, closing the door behind us.

It was warm in the shop and after a glance around, I realized it was thanks to the heater in the corner. One wall of the shop had wreaths in all kinds of styles hanging from top to bottom. Some looked traditional with big red bows at the bottom and others were a little more styled with red baubles. The opposite wall held metal wreath frames and Styrofoam circles. So, processing old trees meant turning them into wreaths.

"You're a wreath maker?" I asked and approached the table. There was a metal box full of tree branches and another full of Christmas ornaments.

"From seven to nine, yes," Jared said. "I thought you could help."

"So, to keep my secret, you want me to help the family business?" I could tell from his expression that he didn't really have a firm answer.

"For now," he said.

Ugh. Was this the deal? I'd be forever indebted to Jared McAdams to do whatever he needed at a given moment?

"How about, you teach me how to make a wreath and I design it however I want to?" I asked, looking over the baskets of supplies. There were ribbons, baubles, and bells of all kinds of colors, and it didn't seem like they'd ever used any of the non-traditional options.

Jared looked at me nervously. "Promise you're not trying to sabotage me?"

"Pinky promise," I said, referring to yesterday's conversation. I held up my right pinky and he smirked.

"You can put that away, Elsa. I believe you."

"My name is Madison," I corrected.

"Madison..." he let the words tail off, gesturing for me to continue.

"Sinclair."

"Oh. I see." He went back behind the table again and started adding tree branches to the wreath he'd been working on.

"What does *that* mean?"

He snorted. "When I was little, too young to work here, I had a paper route. Your family lives in the big cabin at the top of the mountain. I saw you do a backflip on the deck one time."

"I'm starting to rethink the whole you not being creepy thing," I said and approached the table.

Jared pulled a wire frame out of my reach and replaced it with a Styrofoam circle.

"You can use this for your little experiment," he said.

I took it from him despite my annoyance and then went to the end of the table to look at all the supplies.

"So, cheerleader or gymnast or martial artist?" he asked.

"Cheerleader," I said. "I grew up competing with a gym in Denver and I cheered on the school team at Heritage City Academy."

Jared let out a whistle as he affixed a red bauble to the wreath with a piece of wire. "What do you do now?"

I picked up a bright-pink ornament only to see another a few shades lighter further in the pile. "I study fashion design at Kent State University. What about you?"

"I study business at the University of Colorado."

I had picked up so many baubles in different shades of pink that I had to start a pile on the table so I could go back for more. I was deciding between adding in a few silver or rose gold baubles when I realized he'd said business.

"I want to own my own fashion line," I said and looked up from the baskets. "What's your plan?"

He added another bauble, this one silver, before looking up at me. "I want to expand the mercantile. I don't really know what that will look like, but I think there's a lot of potential here with the store in the barn and our location. Crescent Peak sees so many tourists in the winter, but there are still tons that come and camp in the summer months and we don't offer as much during those seasons. We could though. I just haven't decided what that would be."

I nodded and looked back down at the baskets, thinking

through my design so far. What I really wanted was to add more natural elements. I found a basket of pinecones. I added several of those to my pile. I wanted more, but there wasn't anything else organic. I'd have to make something. I took a new roll of pale-pink ribbon and sat it on the table before going back for another in the same color.

"That's a big bow you got there," Jared said.

I shook my head. "I'm going to use it to make roses."

He smirked. "Creative."

I gave him a little curtsy and then started to arrange my elements to get an idea for the design before I started. We worked in silence for a while, the only sound was the low hum of the heating unit. I had a whole wreath of evergreen when he spoke again.

"Why Kent?"

My hand stilled before I could add the pink bauble. No one had ever asked me why I chose the university I had. The people in my family's circle just knew it was a great school for fashion, but no one ever asked me any more questions about the decision, so I never had to fess up to the other reason I chose it.

"It felt far enough from home to avoid the family name."

It was Jared's turn to hesitate. "Maybe I was being a little presumptuous…"

"You assumed I was a stuck-up rich girl whose privilege gets them whatever they want and out of whatever they deserve," I said. It was a phrase Rainy used from time to time to remind me that I was different from the Elon Musk and Kardashians of the world. I was still filthy rich, though.

Jared laughed. "Yes, but I've never heard a stuck-up rich girl admit to it before."

I ignored the compliment and started adding various shades of pink ornaments to my wreath. He let me work in silence until I had added a few pinecones and started to turn the pink ribbon into roses.

"What are you hoping to do in the future?"

I'd already told him about going to Kent to avoid my parents. How much in depth did I dare to go?

"Own a clothing line. The mercantile could use some work, you know?"

He smiled and sprayed something over his wreath, probably some chemical to make the evergreen last longer. He added it to the wall of finished wreaths where it blended in immediately with the other red, gold, and silver pieces.

"What is that bubblegum monstrosity you're working on over there?" he asked.

I waved him away before he could approach me. "Real art pushes boundaries."

"Christmas is red and green."

"Just because something is tradition, doesn't mean it's right."

He laughed. "Touché."

"I know I'm right," I said and added the final rose to the wreath. "It doesn't mean that I know what I'm doing all the time or that what I make is good, but I know that much."

I lifted the wreath to get a better look at it. Jared moved closer, stopping at my shoulder to look at it. I looked at his face as he studied it. I almost laughed at the curious look on his face.

"It's different," he said.

"You don't like it," I laughed.

"No, no. It's not that," he assured me and took the wreath from me. I felt pride swell in my chest as he added it to the wall of finished wreaths. "Can you make one with different blues? My mom likes blue."

"Sure," I told him and took another Styrofoam circle. "But you have to promise that you'll add the pink one to your inventory and not just dismantle it or put it in some storeroom."

Jared held up his right pinky finger. "I swear."

"So, if I come in tomorrow, it will be in the barn with a price tag on it?"

He smiled and held up his left pinky finger. "I promise."

"Blue it is."

"I'm not selling the blue one though, just so you know. That one is going on the door of the house," he told me and went back to his station. I noticed that this time he grabbed ornaments in different shapes, all red, but at least he was expanding his knowledge a little.

"I know," I said as I gathered baubles in different shades of blue. "Your mom likes blue."

Chapter 5

I WENT STRAIGHT to the diner after I left McAdams Mercantile. The diner was the only place in the entire town that served breakfast, lunch, and dinner. It was known in town as "the diner" but was technically called Crescent Peak Diner.

Margot and Marlee were sitting at a table together when I got there. Margot had a glass of water on the table and Marlee had a mug of coffee, her one vice if you didn't include carrying a book with her everywhere.

"Have a nice time?" Margot asked.

"Yeah. It was fun," I said and slipped into the booth next to her. Our waitress appeared next to me to take my drink order. Water with lemon and some mint, if they had it. They always had mint.

"Where were you?" Marlee asked, sipping the black liquid. I didn't like coffee at all, but how she drank the stuff straight was beyond me. Just one more thing I didn't understand about her.

"Coffee with a few other witches," I said with a shrug, taking a menu from the table and using it to hide my face before it could betray me. I never was a good liar. I was the worst, actually. You'd think after sneaking out to all those parties in high school, I would've learned a thing or two. Nope.

"Your Instagram picture was cute," Margot said as the waitress returned with my water and saved me from any more conversation about where I was this morning. Margot ordered the protein bowl, Marlee a plate of waffles, and I ordered an omelet.

"Marlee won a hundred bucks for a short film," Margot said.

Marlee turned red immediately.

"It was a screen recording. It wasn't like I had a cameraman or anything," she said.

Margot pulled out her phone and started to type away, prompting Marlee to word vomit about the entire project. It was a screen recording where the computer user pulled up a YouTube video of some moody music and started to write a poem in Word Document, but they kept getting interrupted by text messages from someone you find out they have a crush on. You learn as the song plays that the person is their best friend, and the poem explains that she'd been in love with him since they were little, and just never knew how to approach the topic. Marlee told me that by the end of the song, which was also the end of the video, the computer user deletes the entire poem, and the song finishes with the short list of credits flashing over the black screen.

"I was going to show her," Margot said in a whiny tone. She lowered her phone and promised to send me a link so I could watch the whole thing later.

"Sounds cool," I told her.

Marlee shrugged. "It was just something I put together on a Saturday when Mom and Dad were both gone for business trips."

"They left you alone?" Margot asked, appalled.

I groaned, mostly at her reaction. Mom and Dad used to leave us alone all the time. It never seemed like a big deal though because we were in charge of Marlee. No one ever talked about the fact that maybe someone needed to be in charge of teenage *us*. We had a list of emergency contacts and Margot's friend's mom who would drive us to school each morning.

"I'm almost eighteen. It's not like they were overseas," Marlee said. "Mom was in California and Dad went to Tennessee. It was just a week and Dad was home a few days early."

"Still…" Margot said.

I groaned. "We could spend the rest of our lives talking about Mom and Dad's workaholic tendencies, but I choose to move on with my life."

"How? What's your plan?" Margot asked with a challenging tone.

I stuck my tongue out at her. "I am going to own my own clothing line."

"Watch out Coco Chanel," Marlee said under her breath.

I resisted the urge to kick her under the table.

"What are you two planning on doing?" I asked.

Margot and Marlee exchanged glances as though deciding who should go first. Neither of them spoke. Marlee looked bored with the conversation. She looked out the window and then glanced down at her phone.

"Professional soccer," Margot said as though it was obvious. It was kind of obvious. She was good, always had been. She was a freshman with a strong shot at starting on the UCLA team. Dad sent us all a group text of an article that listed her as an upcoming superstar in the making.

"What if you don't get a good team?'

"I'll play whatever," she said with a shrug. "I just want to play."

"What about you, Marlee?" I asked.

She looked up from her phone and surprise flitted across her face.

"Law school, of course," Margot blurted. "How long has it been since you called her?"

I shushed her, not caring that the couple a table over had turned to glare at us. That was Margot's fault for trying to make me look bad. "She can tell me herself. She doesn't need a spokesperson."

"Well, she might when she's a senator," Margot shot back.

"Is that what you want to do, be a senator?" I asked.

Marlee's cheeks were turning pink from all the debate. She hated attention. When we were little, I always tried to talk my sisters into putting on shows with me. Margot would go along with it and let me call the shots. Marlee never did. She used to point the beam of flashlights at us like spotlights or write the playbills we would hand out to our parents before the play curtain call.

"Something like that," she said. "Law school."

I didn't press her for more information because the waitress came with our food, and I hadn't realized how hungry I was. The morning had flown by. Not only was talking with Jared kind of interesting but making wreaths was fun. He asked me to come at the same time tomorrow and though I was a little irritated that he wouldn't just admit that he wanted me to work at the mercantile in exchange for keeping my secret, I said yes.

We had finished eating and were waiting for the waitress to bring us the bill when the door opened, and Winnie Maxwell walked in with the same sorority sisters she'd been with at the rink. Thankfully, the hostess led them to the opposite side of the diner. They were all dressed, yet again, in sorority pullovers and leggings. Winnie had her curls in a half-up, half-down do.

"Can I get a coffee to go?" Marlee asked our waitress, obviously not noticing my discomfort. The waitress left us without the bill to get my little sister her stupid coffee and I tried using Instagram as a distraction. I always ignored the suggestions, but this time I clicked on Winnie's profile when I saw it come across as a suggested follow.

Her Instagram page was carefully curated, looking like any other sorority girl's feed with game-day photos and themed-party selfies with other similar-looking sorority sisters. I didn't see a single photo going back the last few months of any boy who might have been her boyfriend. I clicked out of her feed only to see a post that she must've made just moments ago in the diner.

She and her two friends were all smiling in front of the sign for Crescent Peak. The caption read *snow sisters* and had the Greek letters for their sorority. I clicked on the geotag for Crescent Peak and found myself scrolling through a combination of tourist photos and promotional ads for the businesses in town. I stopped when I saw one for McAdams Mercantile. I wondered if Jared had an Instagram account and before I could decide if looking him up was a good idea, I searched for his name and his brown eyes stared back at me from his profile picture.

His bio said he was studying business at the University of Colorado, worked at McAdams Mercantile, loved the outdoors, and had hiked sixteen fourteeners in Colorado. I had to do a Google search to figure out that a fourteener was one of fifty-eight mountain peaks in the state that were taller than fourteen thousand feet.

I had just returned to his Instagram profile when the waitress finally returned with Marlee's coffee and our bill.

"Keep the change," Margot said and handed over a hundred-dollar bill. The waitress was taken aback by the amount but accepted and wished us a good day. I only had just a split moment to decide what to do. I wanted to scroll through his account, but I had just mulled over what was considered creepy all morning. So, I added him as a friend instead and then immediately shoved my phone into my purse and hoped that he wouldn't mention it tomorrow.

I saw Winnie glance our way as we left and I pretended not to notice, not feeling like I could fully breathe until we were outside in the cool air. It had started to snow, soft flakes floating around us as we walked to the back of the lot where our cars were parked.

"Want to go for a drive?" I asked. "I can drop you off for the SUV later."

Margot offered an apologetic smile. "I need to get a few practice hours in."

"I thought you used the gym this morning."

She nodded. "I did. I need to touch a ball though, do some drills coach told me about."

I looked at Marlee who practically shrank under my stare.

"I have an AP paper I want to write over the break. The due date overlaps with my debate team schedule in January," she said.

Well, taking a drive by myself didn't sound like much fun.

"Maybe another day," I said and pulled my keys from my purse. "I should probably take a note from Marlee's book and plan for my classes next semester anyway."

Neither of them protested and we all got into the cars: Marlee and Margot in the SUV and me in my Jeep. The drive to the cabin from Crescent Peak wasn't long. It was nice to look at all the small-town buildings decorated for the season. The trees outside the community building were decked out with orna-ments and lights. Some of the houses a little farther up the mountain had the same metal snowflake over the front door, an unspoken nod to our witchy heritage.

The three of us pulled into the garage at the same time. Mom and Dad were nowhere to be found when we went inside, probably in their respective offices working on who knew and who cared what.

"Maybe we can do something tomorrow," Margot said.

Marlee was already at the stairs when she called out her

agreement, not sticking around to make any plans though. Other than going out to eat, what was there for us to do together that we would all enjoy?

The thought came to me before Margot could fully turn toward the stairs.

"We should go shopping for dresses for the gala!" I said.

Margot looked back at me. "I thought you had a dress."

"Yeah, but you and Marlee don't, right?"

The corner of her lips pulled into a smile. "That could be fun."

"I'll make sure you both look good," I told her with a wink.

She reached out and playfully pushed my shoulder before heading upstairs to change into gym clothes again. I moved into the living room. The farthest side of the room was floor-to-ceiling windows overlooking all of Crescent Peak going down the mountain. It was beautiful, especially with the snow swirling outside the way it was now.

I went to my room for my laptop and spent the afternoon working on my website in front of the windows. I had products on my website, but none of them were available yet. It allowed me to play with the organization of the website while still getting analytics since the website was live. I had always planned on officially opening shop once I'd graduated, but the more research I did and the more clothing I designed, the more confident I was that the business was closer to being ready for launch than my graduation date was.

I hadn't seen her walk by, but there she was.

Margot was on the front lawn with a soccer ball perched on her hip. She sat it down in the snow and faced the side of the garage. She held out a hand and snow shot from her palm and hit the side of the garage with a *splat*, leaving behind a snowy circle on the log siding. She used the mark for target practice, kicking the soccer ball from different positions on the lawn and at different distances until she was consistent at each.

I'd lost track of time watching her. Marlee passed by me and sank into the chair across the coffee table from me. She opened her laptop and started typing again, not saying a word. I was glad for the company. Often, it felt like it was just the three of us in the great big world. Everyone wanted what our family had, but no one really understood the complexity of that except us.

At least, there was that.

Chapter 6

THE NEXT MORNING, I went to the mercantile a little early, planning to hold Jared to his word and see if my wreath was hanging in the barn.

"Morning, Madison," Mark greeted me when I walked in.

"Mark," I returned with a wave and looked over the wall of wreaths to the left of the entrance. They were all the same model, red with silver baubles, aside from two which had gold instead of silver ornaments. It shouldn't have bothered me. Not as much as it did, but my stomach sank, and I scanned the rest of the room in case there was another display somewhere.

"Here to shop or here for Jared?" Mark asked me, breaking my focus.

"Um, Jared," I said. Mark pointed me toward the trees out back and I went straight for the rows before he could give me further instructions. I followed the loud *thunk* that echoed around the field, assuming I would find Jared responsible for the racket. Just like I thought, I found him at one of the farthest rows, a third of the way down, with an axe in hand.

He let out a grunt as he swung, the head of the axe sinking into the divide he'd already made as though he'd done it a thousand times. He must've been at this all morning because his sleeves were rolled up and he didn't have a hat on today. He raised an arm to swipe at his brow when he noticed me and smiled.

"Didn't think you'd be here for another thirty minutes," he said. He lowered the ax to his side, leaning on the head like a cane.

"I thought you said you would put my wreath in the shop," I said and crossed my arms.

"I did," he said.

"It's not there," I told him. "Did you move it?"

His smile widened and he moved closer. "I put it out first thing this morning and it sold an hour later. You were right about us needing to push the status quo."

I felt my stomach twist with satisfaction, but I wasn't about to admit it to him.

"Does that mean I'm off the hook for this whole keeping secrets thing?" I asked, motioning between us.

He shook his head, amused. "Not a chance, Elsa."

"It's Madison," I corrected. If he called me that just one more time or made some cheesy Ice Queen joke...

"What do you have planned for me today?" I asked and clapped my hands together.

He raised the axe toward me, but I didn't move. No way. No way was I chopping a tree down. I'd probably chop my foot off by mistake.

"Relax," he said as I took the axe. "I'll do the chopping. You just keep talking."

I snorted. "You brought me out here to talk to you?"

"The time passes quicker when you're around," he said and motioned for me to move back. I did as I was told, but there was little opportunity to talk as he started swinging again. Once he made a decent-sized wedge at the base of the tree, he held the axe out to me again. Before I could ask if he wanted me to finish the job, he picked up a handsaw.

"Why not just use a chainsaw?" I asked, weighing the axe between both hands.

Jared put a piece of tarp over the snow and then knelt on it. "It's not as satisfying to me." He started to saw away at the tree until it began to lean. He moved back and the five-foot tree fell between us.

"Why cut these trees anyway? Don't you usually let people come and pick them out first?"

He smiled. "You're pretty concerned about our business practices."

"Call me curious."

"Well, for a fashion major you sure got a lot to say about trees." He smiled as he reached for the axe. He told me we were going to cut a few more and then go for a tractor with a trailer to pick them up.

He took almost the same number of swings for each tree before switching to the hand saw. After the fourth tree, he stood up with the saw in one hand and the other extended for the axe.

"Let's go get that trailer," he said.

I walked beside him, heading for a smaller red barn to the right of the field. I could see the tractor in question parked in front with a red trailer attached.

"What's the best part of this job?" I asked.

He left me next to the tractor to go into the barn, emerging seconds later with a set of keys.

"Providing a service," he said.

I guess that was true for my website, too. I wanted to make quality clothing available to as many people as I could. Quality and cute. Two things that didn't always go together, but totally could.

"Have you ever driven a tractor?" he asked with a laugh. I wish the answer wasn't so obvious.

"Why me?" I asked. Jared climbed onto the tractor and took a seat. The engine let out a rough hum as he turned the key. He patted his lap and that's when I understood what he meant.

"It's a much smoother a ride from up here than back in the trailer," he said.

Those really were the only options. Not only would the trailer likely be a bumpy trip, but the bed wasn't the cleanest. Without a word, I approached the tractor and assessed it for the best foothold. Jared held out a hand and I took it, not needing to do much else and he practically dragged me into place.

He was a large enough guy that I felt like a toddler sitting on his lap. He placed my hands on the steering wheel, which was surprisingly thin compared to the Jeep's. The entire machine vibrated under us and that only got worse as Jared showed me where the controls were, and we started to move.

"Slow down. We're just going around the row, not around a racetrack," Jared laughed.

I elbowed him but followed his instructions. He reminded me to give the tractor a little extra room to turn with the trailer behind us when we reached the end of the row. I gave it a little too much gas when we reached a low spot in the field, and I was nearly bucked off his lap. He wrapped his arms around my waist and my head flew back into his. He groaned and when he raised his hands to assess the damage, he knocked my hat off and the left tractor wheel rolled over it.

"I think I'll walk," I said and hopped down. My pink hat was smeared with dirty snow and some kind of tractor grease from the tractor that I was sure would be there forever. I turned the hat over in my hands before tucking it into my coat pocket.

"I'm sorry, Madison. Take my hat."

I caught the beanie when he tossed it to me. "It's not your fault. I was driving."

"Yeah, but I put you behind the wheel," he said and offered his hand again. "I promise I'll do the driving this time."

I let out a sigh and let him pull me up again. He eased the

tractor the rest of the way. Once we reached the four trees lying in the aisle, we got down and worked together to load them into the trailer. Jared tied them down using the tarp and then we were back in the driver's seat again, though I declined to do the driving this time.

We stopped at the back of his silver truck, which he had parked near the small barn. I helped him transfer all four trees from the trailer to the bed of the truck. He covered them again with a tarp and then went to the driver's door before he looked back at me.

"How much time do you have?" he asked.

I paused to think of a good excuse, long enough that it was obvious that I didn't have one. I didn't have any friends up here to visit anymore. Margot was probably busy training and Marlee was doing whatever Marlee did all by herself.

"Where are we heading?" I asked.

"Hop in and I'll show you," he said and got in the truck.

I went around to the driver's side. His truck was tall, so I had to use the seat to climb in. He was already cranking the heat, which only filled the cab with the smell of the outdoors. He turned the radio on and then lowered the volume. The music was soft, a little folksy, and fit the mood of the light snow falling across the windshield.

"You're not going to drive me into the woods and then leave my body in a ditch, are you?" I asked as we bounced over the field and toward the main road.

Jared laughed. "Well, now that you discovered my master plan. I'll just have to try harder next time."

"You are… goofy."

"Like Mickey Mouse's friend or…?"

"No," I laughed, glad that we finally reached the road, and the ride was much smoother. "Like dad jokes."

"Dad jokes are wholesome. What's wrong with being wholesome?" Jared teased.

"Nothing. It was just an observation."

"Well, you're pretty nice— for a rich witch, that is." He glanced sideways at me before looking back at the road. He kept on the fork that would take us down the mountain and into Heritage City. Surely this wouldn't be an all-day kind of trip, though it wasn't like I had any other plans for the day. Jared was so easy to talk to that the day would probably fly by. He was exactly the kind of person you wanted to take a road trip with. He kept it interesting.

Jared was a terrible singer, but that didn't keep him from singing once we switched the station to old rock ballads. He was so unembarrassed that I joined in after a while. Once we reached Heritage City, he turned off the highway and one last turn put us in the busy parking lot of a retirement home.

"They're supposed to have volunteers to help me unload," he said as we got out. As though on cue, two middle-aged men propped open a double door and a group of men began filing out. The oldest man of the bunch approached us with a big smile. The nametag over his breast told me they were from the local moose lodge. Without prompting, they started to unload the trees and file back inside the building like ants at a picnic.

"Is there an event or something?" I asked Jared as we followed the men. They went in different directions with the trees once we reached a large sitting room in the middle of the building. All four of the trees were being raised in the corners of the room. In the middle, a group of high school students dressed in green T-shirts were busy separating Christmas lights.

"Every year, we donate four trees to the retirement home. The moose lodge helps us and then does karaoke— all Christmas songs— once everything is all set up. Heritage City High School's student council decorates the trees and distributes gifts for the residents," Jared said as a group of blonde girls in green T-shirts ran past us wearing a string of blinking lights like feather boas.

Just seeing the cheery chaos in the room made me smile.

"This is all…" I looked at Jared as though he would fill in the blanks. "*Wholesome.*"

He smirked. "What do snowmen eat for breakfast?"

I could tell by his goofy grin that he was about to tell a joke.

"Frosted flakes," he answered.

We didn't stay very long, just long enough to thank everyone for helping and talk with some of the staff members. Jared said that he usually stayed for the karaoke, but we were supposed to get heavy snow that afternoon and he didn't want to drive the mountain roads in those conditions.

We sang a little more on the ride back, not stopping until we saw the sign for McAdams Mercantile a few miles away from the entrance.

"So, what is it like being a witch?" Jared asked.

I opened my mouth to say it wasn't very different from not being a witch, but that wasn't true. I told him there was the having winter powers part. We also had rituals we did for the winter solstice, which our community at Crescent Peak always did at the gala. There was a traditional dance done by the elders and then the rest of us. It was supposed to be symbolic of time passing and ensure that our powers stayed all year. Magic didn't work that way, so it wasn't like I'd stop being a witch if I didn't dance at the winter solstice, but even witches have their superstitions.

"I'm a terrible dancer," Jared said as we pulled into the driveway. "I don't have a lick of rhythm."

I laughed as he parked the truck next to my Jeep. "I figured that out during the first verse of Livin' on a Prayer."

Instead of going into the barn, he led me around it to the tree field.

"I forgot the axe and saw in the field, didn't I?" he said. He let out a long sigh and we changed course from the workshop to the row of trees we'd spent the morning between. As we approached the row, he slowed his pace. His expression changed. He had that hill between his brows that he had the other day when he was thinking deeply.

I ignored it and went with him to retrieve the tools. He picked up the axe first and stopped, looking over the next tree. To my surprise, he started chopping away at the trunk until there was just a small section holding the tree upright.

"Come here," he said. "Want to try sawing it yourself?"

I shook my head. "I'd probably end up stuck under it even if I did manage to cut it down."

He smiled and shook his head. "Trust me. I'll make sure you aren't."

I paused for a moment before I joined him. I took the saw in my right hand and positioned the blade against the crack in the tree. Jared put his arms around me to adjust my grip, changing my hold on the saw entirely. I was just about to mention that I was right-handed when I caught a whiff of him on my right shoulder. It was a spicy smell like cinnamon. My eyes met his for a moment before I heard someone gasp behind us.

"Sorry. I didn't—"

As we sprang apart, I looked back at Winnie Maxwell. Her shocked expression faded to a glare. She looked mad, like I was somewhere I wasn't allowed to be. Something about the situation was strange. I looked at Jared who gave her a meek wave.

"Hey," he said.

Winnie groaned, muttered something under her breath, and stormed past us. I whipped around to watch her go, waiting until she was halfway down the row of trees to say anything.

"Do you know that girl?" I asked.

Jared shrugged, but the fact that he wouldn't meet my gaze and he looked more serious than I'd yet to see him, confirmed it.

"You know her," I said. "Are you with her?"

"No," he blurted, cheeks turning pink. "I used to be."

Oh my God.

Oh no.

I started walking to the barn, my phone in my hand and Instagram already opened as I typed in his name. This time, I started to scroll through the photos. I didn't have to scroll far before I found a photo of him on a college campus with a to-go cup of coffee in his hand, standing next to Winnie Maxwell who smiled back at the camera.

No.

I turned to face him, and he stopped walking after me.

"Were you using me to piss her off?" I asked, the words flying from my lips.

He looked back with an apologetic expression. "Yes, but I want you to know that I do like you. I think you're really smart and nice and not anything like I thought you'd be."

I started walking back to the barn before he'd even finished talking. He ran around me, cutting me off at the end of the row.

"I've been having a great time hanging out with you. Haven't you?"

I wanted to deny it, but I couldn't. It was easy talking to Jared.

"Yeah. I was," I said, with emphasis on *was.*

He didn't even blink at the sass. "What if we keep this up?"

"Are you asking me out?"

"No. No, I mean…" He hesitated like he was struggling to find the words. "Let's just keep this going. I think you're a lot of fun, but…"

I let out a groan. "You want her back, don't you? I know that she broke up with you."

"It's that obvious?" he asked, holding his hands out. His tone was exasperated as if he'd just missed the winning touchdown at the championships. As much as I thought Winnie was a horrible person, I did feel a little bad for him. How someone like him would ever date her though…

"Was that your entire plan? Get me to pretend to date you to make your ex-girlfriend jealous just so you won't tell anyone about me?" I asked.

He didn't respond and he didn't need to.

"Wow," I said and turned on my heel. I ignored his calls for me to stop and his insisting that it wasn't his plan. I walked all the way through the barn and straight to my Jeep. When I looked up before I backed out of the spot, he was standing at the end of the parking lot.

Watching me leave was all I would let him do.

Chapter 7

I DROVE around Crescent Peak to try cooling off, even rolling down my windows to feel the winter air and let it connect with my powers. Normally, this would put me in a kind of witchy trance, but I was far from Zen. After going down all the streets that I could, I headed up the mountain for the cabin.

The snow had started to pick up, leaving a light dusting over the road. It was heavy enough that Margot wasn't even outside anymore practicing. I parked next to the SUV in the garage, the door rolling shut behind me as I gathered my purse and keys and went inside.

I tossed my purse and keys on the kitchen counter, not noticing Margot sitting on the other side with a bowl of noodles.

"Bad morning?" she asked, her eyes going to the top of my head. "Whose hat is that?"

I ripped Jared's beanie from my head.

"I don't want to talk about it," I said.

"Did you eat?"

"Nope."

"I'm having a late lunch. I made ramen from scratch. Grab a bowl."

"Nope," I said and went for the stairs. Maybe it was petty, but

I didn't care that I was short with my sister, and I didn't care that my stomach chose that moment to growl. I went straight to my bedroom and into the attached bathroom.

I tossed Jared's beanie onto the counter and set my phone on top of it. My face was flushed with embarrassment, and it only grew worse as I thought about the look on Winnie's face. She was probably gossiping to her friends right now about me right now.

Why did I care, anyway? What was it about Winnie that got so under my skin that I would revert back to the shallow girl I was in high school? I didn't do those things anymore. Other than dressing up and putting effort into my appearance, I wasn't at all the same girl as I was then.

I combed my fingers through my curls, trying to add a little volume at my roots where the beanie had flattened them. I could smell that same spicy cologne that hung on Jared's skin on my hair and hands. I washed my hands and then sprayed some perfume over myself.

When I went back to my bedroom, a bowl of ramen sat on the desk in front of the window overlooking the lawn. The steam from the bowl had formed a little halo of fog over the window, obscuring the spot on the lawn where Margot usually practiced. I changed out of my clothes and into a pair of sweatpants and a Kent State sweatshirt. It smelled like Rainy's lavender laundry soap, which reminded me that I forgot to switch the towels from the washing machine to the dryer before I left for the airport. Great.

I went back to the bathroom for my phone to warn Rainy about the mildew smell that would surely invade our apartment while we were both home for the holidays. An Instagram notification blinked back at me when I picked up my phone, the username reigniting the frustration I felt.

Jared McAdams started following me.

I exited the app and typed my apology out to Rainy who

would be the first one back to our apartment in a few weeks and went to the desk to eat my lunch.

DAD MADE tacos and we ate at the table as a family for the first time since we'd all been home together.

"I bought a few of those gingerbread house kits," Dad told us as he took the rest of Mom's dinner and scraped it onto his plate. "I thought we could all make our own after dinner."

"Oh! We could watch a Christmas movie," Margot said on her way to take her plate to the sink. She dropped it off and went to the sitting area for the remote.

"As long as it's not Elf, I'm in," Marlee said.

Margot looked away from the TV screen. "What's wrong with Elf?"

"It's okay, I guess," Marlee said. "Maybe it would make for good background noise, actually."

"Don't worry. We'll save the serious films for you to analyze for later," I said.

Mom and Dad were in the kitchen, so Marlee got away with the two middle fingers she sent my way. I returned the favor by blowing her a kiss.

Mom came to the table with a baking tray stacked with gingerbread pieces and Dad followed with plastic shopping bags of different kinds of candy to decorate with. Once Margot had *Elf* playing on the TV, we divided out the house pieces and worked in silence to build our masterpieces.

I hadn't realized how disconnected our little family bonding activity really was until I looked up from my finished ginger-bread house, complete with a thatched roof of pretzel sticks, and realized that no one was paying any attention to anyone else. It was just all of us sitting together, doing separate things. Had it always been like this?

"I'm going to shower," I announced.

No one tried to stop me as I went to the stairs. I went to the bathroom and scrolled through Instagram while the water heated up. My feed was full of family photos now that most of my friends were home. Rainy posted a photo of her sitting on the stairs of her parents' house with the family dog, a golden retriever wearing a pair of reindeer antlers.

I went to my own feed. The photo I posted this morning had a record number of likes. The first few comments were from spam accounts asking me to send the photo to some blog or DM them to check out their scammy business opportunity. Rainy left a string of white rabbit emojis in the comments as a reference to my *snow bunny or snow hunny* caption. A few other college friends told me I looked fierce and to have a great winter break.

I closed my phone when I noticed the steam collecting on the mirror. The warm water felt nice on my skin and just like always, I felt so much better once I had washed and was dressed in my flannel pajama set. I braided my damp hair and pinned it at the nape of my neck so it would curl overnight.

I had only just started to work on a new T-shirt design on my laptop when a knock came at my door.

"Come in," I called out.

The door opened and Margot peeked her head in.

"Don't worry," she said. "It's just me."

She shut the door behind her when I closed my laptop. She sat at the end of the bed and crossed her legs underneath her.

"Were you with a boy today?" she asked. Margot never beat around the bush. If you wanted to share secrets, Margot was your girl. If you wanted blunt honesty, Marlee never failed to deliver it.

"Yeah, but not like that. We just met," I told her. How much should I tell her? Margot wouldn't tell a soul, but I didn't want to get her lecturing me about using my magic in public.

A girly smile spread across her face.

"Okay. Have you been talking? Is this a boy you met online, someone you matched with on an app?"

I tossed one of my throw pillows at her. I'd never been on a dating app before. I had enough gross interactions with boys in real life and I didn't need any of it online.

"I met him at the mercantile," I told her. There weren't many shops in Crescent Peak, so everyone went to the mercantile. It didn't really narrow down the pool at all.

"Is that what you were mad about earlier?"

"Yes and no."

"Did he do something?" Margot asked, straightening up.

I shook my head. "No. He's fine."

"So, why were you mad?"

I wasn't sure anymore. Now that I had the time to think about it, Jared is just a broken-hearted boy who was looking for ways to make things right with his ex-girlfriend. We all said stupid things because of love at some point in our lives. He wasn't being creepy when he suggested we pretend to date. Desperate, maybe. But not creepy.

"He just got out of a relationship, and I don't want to be anyone's rebound girl," I said.

Margot laughed. "You're not the kind of girl a boy uses as his rebound. You're the prize, Madison."

I should've just accepted the compliment, but I rolled my eyes instead.

"I don't worry about that kind of stuff anymore."

"You just said that you didn't want to be a boy's rebound," Margot laughed.

Okay. Good point.

"Well, maybe I just don't want to be used to make someone else feel better," I said.

Margot nodded. That's what this was. Jared wanted me to pretend to date him so he wouldn't look sad and lonely. Sorry to break it to you, Jared. A fake relationship wouldn't make you feel less sad and lonely. You'd just feel sad and lonely while also being with someone.

"Do you like him?" she asked.

I did before I knew he was the kind of guy that dated the Winnie Maxwells of the world.

"Yeah. He's nice," I said with a shrug.

Margot hesitated, looking around my room in thought. Her eyes landed on my open closet and the white gown that hung there.

"You should ask him to the gala," she said and then turned back to me. "He is a warlock, right?"

I wasn't about to get into that mess.

"I don't know if I want to be with him. Why would I ask him to go with me?"

She shrugged and said, "If he's hot, he'd give all the snobby witches and nosy elders something to talk about that's not you."

Something clicked in place when she said it. Jared McAdams is hot. That was the only downside to the gala. The young people all showed off what they'd accomplished since the last gala and all the elders bragged on their kids or pried into our personal lives. A date was the only way to prevent all of that. Not to mention, showing up with Winnie's sexy ex-boyfriend would make her mad as hell while impressing everyone in the room. It would be the first gala she'd be attending dateless since we were in school, and no one would care about how involved she was at college or her dumb business degree. It wasn't that I wanted the attention to be on me. I just wanted it off her for once.

"I'll talk with him, but no promises," I said.

Margot smiled. "We can go tux shopping later this week."

She stood up from the bed and I followed her.

"No," I said as she went to the hallway. "But we should go to find dresses for you and Marlee."

Margot let out a dramatic groan. "We will."

"And I'm getting you in heels this year," I called after her down the hall. She waved a hand over her shoulder.

"We'll see about that," she said and disappeared into her bedroom.

Chapter 8

I WOKE up early the next day and got ready. I sprayed a little dry shampoo into my hair and spruced up my curls. I put on a pair of dark-wash jeans and a white sweater that matched Jared's blue and white beanie. I decided to wear my heeled boots, not intending on doing any work in the tree field today, and pulled on my nice winter coat.

A full face of makeup later, I was on my way down the stairs to the garage. Mom was working on her laptop in the living room and Marlee was reading a book in a chair in the corner. Both looked up as I came down the stairs.

"You look nice," Mom said.

I went to her and kissed the top of her head.

"I'll be back for dinner." I grabbed my purse and keys from the kitchen counter and left for the garage. The tires of the Jeep crunched over the thick snow in the driveway. Yesterday's snowfall was heavy enough to cover the lines on the road. I carefully drove down the mountain and through Crescent Peak.

The local bookstore had put a sign out to advertise for a social tomorrow. I made a mental note to tell Marlee about it. On second thought...

I pulled into a parking spot across the street and went to the bookstore. There was a little bell over the doorframe that gave a cute tinkle when I entered.

The shop was a single big room. All four walls were covered in bookshelves tall enough that stepstools were placed around the room for patrons to reach the top shelves. A few tables at the front held candles and other gift items. I went to a table with jewelry first— the only reason I'd ever step foot into a bookstore.

"Looking for anything in particular?" an elderly woman called from the register.

I looked up from the necklace display. "I was going to send my sister a photo of your sign out front for the social, but I decided to come in and look for a gift for her instead."

The woman smiled. I could see the little creases around the corners of her eyes and mouth from here. She was adorable. She could've been anyone's sweet grandmother who always showed up with a plate of cookies and a hundred-dollar bill she'd hand off when your parents weren't looking.

"What does she like?" the woman asked.

I snorted. "Well, she's not the type that goes in a bookstore and starts at the jewelry display."

The woman chuckled and joined me at the table. What drew me in to begin with was the price. The entire table was priced higher than I'd imagine for a bookstore, but as I inspected a few pieces, I could tell they were quality. The company made book-themed pieces. There were novelty earrings in the outline of quills, and necklaces with lockets in the shape of books.

I picked up one of the lockets with a longer chain and then a shorter necklace with a small letter M charm and a crystal pendant, thinking the two necklaces would look cute layered together.

"Well, since you don't know what she might like..." the woman said and offered me a flyer for the social tomorrow. "What do you think she needs?"

Our family didn't need anything. Stability came along with both parents running multi-billion-dollar businesses. What we really needed wasn't money. I let my mind focus on Marlee for once. I didn't understand why she was the way she was, but I knew one thing for sure. My youngest sister had always been so serious, like *always* serious. I'd never seen her laugh hysterically in my whole life. It wasn't that she was a depressed person or anything— at least not that I knew about. She was just... serious.

"Something to make her smile," I told the woman.

She pointed me in the direction of a bookshelf that was filled with books in bright covers, most of them with happy couples on the front. They were adorable, probably the kind of book I'd actually enjoy. I bet Marlee had never even looked twice at this section.

I didn't scan long before I found a Christmas romance that looked promising. Correction, it looked promising to me. Marlee would probably internally scoff when she opened it on Christmas day, but I didn't care. This was me trying to find something we could talk about together.

I picked up the only two copies of *Christmas as We Know It* by Sarah Sutton and went to the register with all my items.

"One for you and one for your sister?" the lady asked as she put all the items into a cute paper bag.

"That's the idea," I said. I thanked for and promised to tell Marlee about tomorrow's social before leaving the shop.

I stood for a moment on the sidewalk. It had started to snow again, the kind of light flakes that made everything look dreamy and tickled the powers buried deep inside of me. I glanced down both sides of the street to make sure no one was around before I let go just a little on the control keeping my powers at bay.

I let out a long sigh and let my powers take over for just a second, long enough for the flakes to dance around me in such a subtle way that most people wouldn't notice the magic. When I reined it in again, I noticed three people leaving the cafe across the street.

Winnie paused when she noticed me, her smile falling until her two friends regained her attention. They all climbed into the SUV parked behind my Jeep and I waited until they'd pulled down the street to cross the road.

HOT CHOCOLATE IN HAND, with whipped cream and sprinkles this time, I walked across the parking lot to the big red barn of the mercantile. It was already busy with tourists, not a single familiar witchy face among the sea of people milling about the room.

It was busy enough that I felt a little bad pulling away any of the employees to ask for Jared. He was probably busy in the field somewhere helping someone pick out their Christmas tree.

I walked through the store instead. Maybe today was just the day to do all my Christmas shopping, because I found candles for Mom and crocheted ear warmers, I thought Margot might like for the winter practices. I was surprised when I reached the home décor corner of the barn to find so many colors other than the red and green that I remembered from earlier in the week.

There were still some wreaths with red and green baubles on them, but the display was started to be overtaken by wreaths with different, non-traditional designs. I saw one with the blue baubles Jared mentioned his mom liked and there were a few others that looked similar to the one I'd made. One wreath even had some roses made of ribbon on them, though they looked more wilted than mine.

I reached up to fluff the ribbon when I heard someone stop behind me.

"Madison Sinclair," the voice said.

I turned to face the dark-haired man that smiled warmly at me. "Mark McAdams."

He chuckled. "Jared told us you made that pink wreath."

"He told me it sold out within hours of being put on the shelf," I said.

Mark nodded. "It did and we asked him to make more. Hey, Jo," he called across the shop.

My cheeks heated as the room of people glanced our way. The store wasn't as full as it had been before. Most of the people had gone to the field to walk the rows, but a few moms with their kids had stayed inside. Joanne looked a little annoyed at first, but when her eyes fell on me her expression grew curious.

"This is the girl that made that wreath," Mark said.

Joanne McAdams came around the register and walked toward us. I don't know what it was. Maybe it was the strong, model walk she had for a forty-something-year-old woman or maybe it was the severe expression on her face, but she was intimidating.

"I thought the idea of a pink wreath was ridiculous, especially when Mark told me it had roses on it," she said before she'd even reached us. I felt my stomach drop into my shoes the way it had when my design professor told me my use of stripes in my mid-term design was unflattering on anyone with any kind of curves.

"I didn't mean to waste any product," I told her.

She snorted, a smile pulling at the right corner of her lips. "I sold it the first hour we were opened. A group of women came in yesterday asking for the same wreath. The lady I sold it to is part of their mom's group. I told them I could get another," she said and looked at me questioningly. "But Jared's roses look like pink burritos."

"I can make another, if you want," I offered.

She nodded. "Jared told me you might not come back."

She started to walk back to the register, the unspoken invitation to follow hanging in the air. Mark and I crossed the barn and watched as she went behind the register and pulled off her red smock.

"We had a little fight. That's all," I said as she folded the smock and stuck it behind the counter. "It was stupid."

When Joanne looked up, it was at Mark. "You think you can handle the store yourself?"

The tone she used and the look she gave him told me she expected him to handle it, whether he could or not. He needed to figure out how.

"Yeah. I've manned the place myself before. It'll be fine."

"Follow me," Joanne told me.

I looked back at Mark, who gave me an encouraging smile. I hurried after Joanne as she left the back of the barn and walked toward the shed. Instead of going inside, we walked right on by. My heart skipped when I realized we were going to the main house a few yards beyond.

The house was painted a light tan color with light blue shutters. When we reached the blue front door, I saw that the wreath with blue baubles was hanging there and a more traditional one was set in one of the two rocking chairs on the porch.

"Are you a tea or coffee kind of person?" Joanne asked as she opened the door and went inside.

I followed her, pausing in the entryway while she went ahead to the kitchen. Just to the right was a formal dining table with enough seats for six people. To the left was a small living room with a big window that overlooked the farm. As much as I wanted to sink into the inviting gray couch, I joined Mrs. McAdams in the kitchen instead.

"I'm still drinking my hot chocolate, but thank you for the offer," I said.

She didn't answer, just continued milling about the kitchen. I looked over the space while she filled the coffee maker. The kitchen was small with heather-gray cabinets and light-blue tiles instead of the granite and marble countertops I was used to.

"Go make yourself comfortable in the living room," Joanne said and waved me off without another look.

I went back into the living room. I turned from the window to see that the opposite wall was a collage of photos and wooden décor pieces, most of them outdoorsy. I moved closer to look over the pictures. They were all family members. I recognized a younger version of Jared, dressed in a green graduation gown, posing next to his mom.

It didn't take me long to discover that Joanne McAdams had always had long, dark hair and must've worn it in a single braid down her back most of the time considering the number of photos she was in with the same hairstyle. I noticed that Mark was in quite a few photos, going back to Jared's childhood. He'd been tall even then.

"Our parents lived here before us," Joanne said, stopping next to me with a mug of coffee in her right hand. "The house was paid off and the farm was doing so well, so I moved here to take over the business full time. Before, Mark and I would drive up during the busy seasons."

"What kind of job did you have then?" I asked.

Joanne moved to the couch and sat down. "Accounting. We lived in Heritage City."

"That's where I grew up," I said and sat on the opposite side of the couch. To answer her questioning gaze, I said, "I went to Heritage City Academy."

She nodded. "Are you in college anywhere?"

I sat my Styrofoam cup on the coffee table. "I study fashion design at Kent State University."

She hesitated with her mug on her lips for a moment before taking a sip.

"That's a good school for that," she said.

I let out a sigh. She was one of the few people I'd spoken to who knew that fact.

"I'm thinking about double-majoring in business. I really like that part of fashion. Creating the clothes is a lot of fun, but there's something super satisfying about creating a business plan. Maybe I'd be better with a marketing minor…"

Joanne let out a laugh. "Go with the double-major in business. It's versatile and you can learn the marketing side of things as you go, especially when you're only twenty-something."

I wasn't sure what to say, so I just nodded and drank my hot chocolate to distract from the silence.

It turned out that Joanne McAdams had once been pretty adventurous. During college, she'd studied abroad in Australia and met a guy there who then traveled the world with her when they were on break from school. She barely finished her degree before giving birth to Jared, which was when the Aussie flew back home and they'd lost touch. Joanne didn't seem too broken up by the fact. She just told me that she used to fly by the seat of her pants when it came to life and hadn't always taken things seriously enough until she had to.

The free-bird attitude reminded me a little of Jared's boyish nature, only he was a little more serious about things. He was the quiet type, I could tell, though it wasn't hard for us to keep a conversation going.

I heard the front door open and a moment later, Jared appeared in the doorway of the living room. He was surprised to see me.

"I, uh, didn't know you were here," he said, looking at me.

"Want to introduce us?" Joanne asked, a hint of amusement pulling at the corner of her lips.

"Um, yeah. Mom, this is Madison Sinclair. She's the one who

made that pink wreath and taught me how to make the blue one you like," Jared told her, motioning to me. His eyes met mine, a hesitant look on his face. He chewed on his lower lip like it would keep him from asking me what I was sure he wanted to.

Why are you here?

"I'm Jared's girlfriend," I told Joanne. She didn't even blink at the words. It was like she'd known them all along.

"You could've warned me that she looks like a city-slicker," Joanne teased Jared, who blushed.

"Mom," he protested.

"Don't worry. She's as smart as she is pretty. I found that out before you politely introduced her to me," Joanne said, doing a double-take and looking over Jared, her expression falling. "You know better than to wear your work boots in the house."

"Sorry. I got distracted," Jared said, flashing a smile my way that made my cheeks heat.

"Go take them off," Joanne said.

"Yes, ma'am."

"If you get mud stuck in the carpet, I'll whoop you."

Jared paused in the hallway, a boyish look coming over his face. "I mean no disrespect, but I'm twice your size."

Joanne tossed a throw pillow at him, unable to contain her smile. It bounced off the wall and fell onto the floor. Jared returned a moment later in his socks.

"There's coffee in the kitchen, if you want to join us," Joanne said.

"Thanks. It's cold out there," he said and started for the carafe.

"Jared, have you been out to service the tractor yet?" Joanne called out, her tone urgent.

"Not yet," he yelled back.

"Put that mug down and go take care of it," Joanne told him. In a quieter voice, she told me, "He threw everything out of whack by racing the tractor, so he can be the one to fix it."

I felt my jaw drop and I quickly covered my embarrassment by lifting my to-go cup to my face. Jared hadn't told me I broke anything when we'd hit that bump. I remembered the beanie on my head now, a kind replacement for my pink hat I'd run over.

"Yes, ma'am," Jared called out. A moment later, the front door closed again, and it was just me and Joanne McAdams.

Chapter 9

IT TOOK Jared into the afternoon to fix whatever it was I broke on the tractor, in which time I'd learned a lot about him from his mom. She told me all about his childhood while she made lunch.

Jared had always been the quiet type. He had a hard time making friends in grade school and took a stuffed dog with him everywhere until he was seven. He was a lineman on the high school football team, which was the last time Heritage City went to state.

"What have you two been talking about?" Jared asked when he came in at two o'clock, remembering to leave his shoes at the door this time.

"I've been telling her all your secrets," Joanne said, her tone so serious that I almost believed her.

Jared gave a dramatic gasp as he leaned against the living room wall. "Don't tell my girlfriend *all* my secrets." He gave me a knowing wink.

"I should probably take over for Mark," Joanne said and stood up from the couch. We'd been there so long that my own were stiff when I stood.

"How about we go walk around Crescent Peak?" Jared asked,

adding "I finished all my duties around here, so unless I'm needed…"

His mom looked mildly annoyed but shook her head.

"Go on," she said and then looked at me. "Has he taken you on a date since you've been here?"

"No."

"Then go to dinner while you're out," she said. "And go clean up first, Jared."

Jared smiled as his mom passed him in the hallway.

"I'll be a minute. Feel free to look around," he said.

"Oh, I fully intend on going through your medicine cabinet. I have to know what kind of guy I'm dating, you know?" I said and followed him down the hallway.

He let out a laugh. "Jokes on you. I'll be in the shower, so unless you plan on joining me—"

He turned red as soon as the words were out of his mouth. I felt my own cheeks burn.

"I'll just wait here," I said and went back to the living room.

Jared was one of those guys that took a suspiciously short shower, but I could tell from the spicy smell when rejoined me in the living room that he'd been thorough. He was wearing a pair of jeans, a gray half-zip pullover, and a cleaner pair of boots than he usually wore.

"I don't really have any date clothes here," he said.

"Jared," I started. "It's not a real date."

He opened his mouth as though to explain but stopped. He pulled a pair of keys from his pocket and flashed them my way.

"How about a coffee first?" He led the way back outside. His silver truck was parked in the gravel driveway.

"I don't like coffee," I said, wrinkling my nose. Sure, the stuff smelled great, but it was so bitter. Even when you put cream and sugar in it, it was bitter.

"Coffee is life," Jared said as we climbed into the cab of the truck. "What are you going to make all those interns bring you while you'll yelling at models during photoshoots?"

I laughed. "Firstly, I won't be yelling like that. Secondly, coffee and cigarettes go together for a reason. They're both bad."

"One will give you concern, the other bad breath?" Jared asked.

"Okay, so maybe not bad in the same way." I said as he laughed. I elbowed him, which was probably not a good idea with him driving. "Whatever." I sat back in my seat.

"What do you order at a café?" Jared asked as we headed up the mountain.

"Hot chocolate with whipped cream and sprinkles."

"Sprinkles?"

"Yeah, like those little chocolate ones," I said as we passed the first buildings in Crescent Peak. "If they don't have those, I ask for little chocolate chips on top. I go back and forth between which is better."

Jared shook his head like I was ridiculous as he parallel parked. "Your café order is basically liquid sugar."

"Sweet, just like my personality," I said and hopped out of the car. He laughed for much longer than I thought necessary at my joke.

There was just one coffee shop in Crescent Peak and like everything else in this tiny town, it was called Crescent Peak Café. So original. So small town. It warmed my heart.

"A large black coffee and a large hot chocolate with whipped cream and sprinkles." Jared ordered for us when we got to the register. I pulled out my wallet as quick as I could and stepped in front of him, ignoring the way his chest felt against my back as I did.

"I got this," I said and handed over my card. The barista swiped it and then we moved to the pick-up corner of the counter. Jared looked back at me like I'd done something heroic.

"I like a girl boss," he said.

"That's my whole masterplan," I told him as I zipped my purse. "Be a boss. Build my own company from the ground up. Might as well act the part."

He smirked and took the coffee from the counter when the barista slid it over. We had to wait a minute longer for the hot chocolate, but it was worth the wait.

"We should walk the town," I said before he could sit down in a cushy armchair near the window. "Maximize our chances at being seen together."

"Good point," he agreed and followed me onto the sidewalk.

We hadn't gone very far when the lights strung around the town lit up the streets. They gave off a warm light, a strong contrast to the chilly air. Jared passed off his coffee for a moment so he could zip up his jacket.

"Does the cold not really affect you guys the same as normal people?"

"Normal people?"

"You know what I mean. Not witch people."

I giggled. "It depends on the witch. There are more than one kind."

He looked back at me with such a shocked expression that I laughed again. Explaining all of this was going to be fun.

"There are different kinds of witches?" he asked.

I shushed him as we got to a busier section of the street. There were lots of couples and families out walking the streets, Christmas music floating from the stores that were still open along the square.

"There are witches for every season: winter, spring, summer, and fall. Men are called warlocks. Our natural powers are related to our seasons. We can use our powers year-round, but they're strongest when we are in season."

Jared snorted. "You say that like you're a flower or some fruit."

I elbowed him, which only made him laugh harder. He led me into a sporting goods store. The front window was full of different brightly colored skis. Jared went for the wall just to the left, the wooden sign overhead labeling it as the hiking section.

"I've never been in here before," I said as he looked at the backpacks.

He turned away from the display in disbelief.

"Your family has a giant cabin in this tiny town, and you've never been in this store after all these years?"

"Nope." I picked up a metal walking pole.

Jared took the pole from me and put it back with the rest before I could impale my foot with it. He went back to looking over the backpacks and then moved to a display of hiking shoes. They looked like the boots I had, only without a heel and the leather around the ankle was a lot thicker and stiffer.

"If you tell me you've never been in here because you're not the athletic type..."

"No. I'm athletic," I defended. "I was a cheerleader in high school. I was on a competitive team in Denver. I'm just not a winter sport kind of person."

I know, it was weird considering winter practically made up my DNA. Jared was now looking at me like I was an alien.

"I thought you liked winter," he said.

I picked up one of the men's boots, surprised at how heavy they were. How could someone trudge through the snow in something this bulky?

"I love the winter, which is why I don't like spending the season being competitive about sports. I like to enjoy it. It's the only time of the year where I actually slow down and take a break." I followed him farther down the wall where he looked over a wall full of clothing.

"You don't have to make it competitive to be a part of it," Jared said and pulled down a pair of pants. They were a light gray and looked like windbreakers but thicker. He handed them to me and I draped them over my arm while he moved on to a new section of hiking boots that had a more colorful selection.

"That's one thing you'll have to get used to about being around me," I told him as he looked over the rack of boots. "I made everything competitive, and I don't lose."

The comment Winnie made to me at the ice-skating rink came to mind.

You can't spell Winnie without W-I-N.

Ugh. I moved closer to Jared, as though our proximity would signal to anyone watching that we were dating. I reinforced the idea in my own head. I'd almost forgotten about our agreement as we'd walked the town.

Jared had stopped walking and I bumped right into him, nearly losing my footing and knocking several of the heavy boots off the rack. Jared laughed at me as I put them back into place, my face flaming.

"You sure you were athletic in high school?" Jared asked.

I tossed the pants at him, and he caught them by the hanger.

"When you're only five-five and you walk into the Jolly Green Giant, you might look a tad uncoordinated."

"I'm hardly the Jolly Green Giant," Jared said with a smirk, placing a light-blue pair of boots on top of the pants over his left arm.

"You're like seven feet tall," I said.

"I'm only six-five." Jared held the stack out to me, but I refused.

"If you're so coordinated," I teased, "then you can carry your own shopping."

He smirked. "You think I could fit in these boots? These are for you to try on."

My stomach dropped. Something about trying on clothes with a boy felt intimate, or maybe it was just the idea of trying on clothes with Jared McAdams, the boy I was supposed to be dating, the six-foot-five man who looked like he spent all day chopping wood. Hell, he did spend all day chopping trees.

"Why?" I asked, the words sounding a little strained when they came out.

"You'll need it when we go hiking," he said, attempting to hand over the stack again.

I took a step back and put my hands up. "Oh no. That wasn't part of the deal."

"How about a new deal then?" Jared drew in closer and lowered his voice. "You agree to a few outdoorsy dates, and you can show me and tell me all about your witchy secrets."

Outdoorsy dates wouldn't exactly be public though. He'd have me walk through the forest for whom? Maybe a couple of deer would spot us. Sure, that'll have the town talking. There was a witchy secret that would put us front and center though.

"New deal," I declared and closed the gap between us. I stood a little straighter. Fat difference that made. I rose onto my tippy toes, which made his boyish smile even wider and made it hard for me to keep my face serious as I made the proposal. "I go on a few outdoorsy dates with you, and you come with me as my date to the Winter Solstice Gala."

"The what?" he asked.

"What do you think it is? It's a gala," I said and took a step back. I held my hands out to except the pile of clothing. He handed it over a little reluctantly.

"I get to pick the tux though," he said. "I hate getting all dressed up, so at least let me pick the most comfortable one."

I was already on my way to the changing room at the back of the store.

"Fine, but everyone wears white. It's required." I shut the door on him and heard him groan.

"I have to find a white tuxedo?" he asked. I heard him mutter something under his breath as I changed into the pants. They were incredibly comfortable and very warm, but they did make a soft swish noise when I moved. That part wasn't so great. They would do for a couple of hikes though.

I changed back into my own pants and moved into the sitting area of the store where Jared was waiting.

"How'd I do?"

"You were spot on with the sizing, which is… concerning," I said and gave him look of warning. He smirked back at me and held onto the hiking pants while I tried on the boots.

"I just took a guess," he promised.

"Well, your guess was wrong about my feet," I said as I slipped into the too-big right boot.

Jared snapped his fingers. "Never was much of a foot guy. Not my thing."

"What is your thing?" I asked as I went to the rack for a half-size down. My stomach twisted really quick. Just because I was pretending to date him didn't mean I had to get personal. It just had to look like we were.

Jared didn't mind the question. He actually let out a laugh.

"I like a nice round butt," he said.

I let out a dramatic groan. "I'll have to start doing a lot of squats then or no one will ever believe we're really together."

I replaced the size seven and a half and took a box of a size seven from the rack. Jared was turning red in the face like the whole conversation was the funniest thing ever.

"No," he told me. "Not a round butt like that. I mean, like, muscular. Like, a girl who hits the gym regularly or is sporty and it shows." His laughter put an end to the conversation, and I joined in when I saw the blush on the blond woman behind the register when she saw the gestures Jared was making.

"Is that why you knew I was a small?" I asked and nodded to the pants draped over his lap.

He smirked again, the laughter building. "Lord knows you're not packing enough to be a medium."

I threw one of the heavy boots at him and he caught it at his chest. After we both recovered, I made sure the hiking boots fit and then bought them and the pants. Jared carried the large shopping bags, doing a little jog down the block and back to show me just how coordinated he was.

Something changed in his face as he slowed his pace on the way back to me. He looked at me such a way that it made everything within me stop. I was aware of how small I was as he stopped in front of me, all six-feet-five feet of him.

"Can I tell you a secret?" Jared asked.

I nodded, muscles tightening when he lifted his free hand to touch my face. He brushed my hair back and I cocked my head to the side as he leaned in, half-expecting to feel the warmth of his lips against my skin when he whispered him my ear.

"My ex just got out of her car down the street," he said.

I exhaled. Every muscle in my body relaxed as I remembered the reality. Jared lingered with his face inches from my neck, probably just long enough to be seen. Then, he straightened up with an awkward smile.

"If you are ever uncomfortable with anything…" he started.

I reached out for his free hand, lacing my fingers in his.

"We told your mom we were going for dinner."

He smiled and we continued down the street toward the diner.

Chapter 10

WHEN I GOT up the next morning, I had a couple notifications from Instagram. They were both notifications of comments on the picture I posted with the Jeep. Jared had answered the question I put in the caption.

SNOW BUNNY OR SNOW HUNNY?

HUNNY, you can hop my way any day.

I WAS SO FLOORED by his comment that I nearly missed the reply attached to it. Margot replied with the same three shocked looking emojis. That explained the texts I also had from her. When I opened the messages there were three different screenshots she'd taken from Jared's Instagram profile. The first was a photo of him sitting on top of the tractor and the second was of him in that same gray half-zip from last night.

Is this the guy???!!

I IGNORED HER MESSAGE, still recovering from the shock of Jared's comment. So, we were really doing this. He was pulling out all the stops.

I remembered that we had exchanged phone numbers at dinner last night and had the phone pressed to my ear in a matter of seconds. It rang so long I almost gave up, a little surprised when he answered.

"Good morning."

"Hi, um, I just thought I'd called." I was beating myself up inside at the awkwardness. Maybe I should've just sent a text instead.

"Ah," he said, drawing out the sound. "You got my message on Instagram."

"What? No. What message?" I asked. Good God, why couldn't I just play it cool and tell him it was funny like a normal person. "I just wanted to see when we were going out again. Do you have time today? I don't mind waiting at the mercantile."

"Yeah. Come here. My mom is under the impression that you're helping around here now. I could use your sense of style with a few wreaths."

"Okay. I'll hop your way. I mean…" I lowered the phone. Dead. I was dead. There was no recovering, and I knew Jared wouldn't let me live it down. I could already hear him howling through the receiver. "Jared," I moaned into the phone.

After a moment, he stopped laughing to speak. "I knew you saw it."

"Give me some time to get ready and I'll meet you there."

"Wear your hiking boots," Jared said a little too excitedly.

Ugh. Not yet.

"Okay. Sure," I said and hung up.

I wore the pants and the boots I bought yesterday, pairing

them with a fluffy sweatshirt with my sorority letters outlined in pink. Jared's beanie matched the pants perfectly. At this rate, and as soft as it was, he was never getting his hat back.

I was quick to leave the cabin and grateful I didn't run into anyone along the way. I wasn't ready to face Margot's teasing yet.

When I got out of the Jeep in the parking lot, Jared was standing outside the big barn doors. Once I reached the walkway to the entrance, he started bunny-hopping toward me. I hurried to meet him and then gave him a shove.

"Not funny," I said, trying to hide my smile.

"I've been waiting here since you called just to do that," Jared said with a laugh.

"So, we're working on wreaths today?" I asked.

"My mom took orders for those women who came looking for that pink wreath you made. I hope you don't mind."

I waved a hand at him. "I'll teach you my ways and it'll take us half the time."

Jared unlocked the door, and we went inside. It was hot, even after being outside in the snow, and I could feel the sweat building.

"Is there a way to turn that down a bit?" I asked.

Jared snorted. "It's down. It's just a small space and it may not look like it, but these walls are insulated."

I took off my coat and laid it across a stool next to a table of wreath frames. Jared tossed his on the floor.

"How many are we making?" I asked.

Jared smiled back at me. It was the kind of smile that made me nervous, like he had a big surprise that he could barely keep in anymore.

"Twelve," he said.

"Twelve?" I asked. "How many friends does this girl have?"

"Four came in looking for the wreath and when my mom took their orders, a few of them wanted extras." He gathered the materials while I took the time to drape his coat over the back of another stool like the civil person I am.

"I think I got most of the technique down. I did make a few," Jared told me as I joined him at the table.

"Yes, I saw your craftsmanship," I said with a laugh. "Your roses are abysmal."

He scoffed but didn't say a word. I took a long piece of pink ribbon and showed him how I started to wrap it with my fingers, explaining how to fan it a little as you continued to wrap.

"Got it," he said.

"You sure?"

"Have some faith and give me a shot." He smiled and started to mimic my technique, showing off how good the rose looked before he'd even finished.

We worked in silence for a while, mostly making pink roses until it was time to assemble a wreath. I was on my second one before he spoke again.

"How about a game of twenty questions?"

I paused with a pink bauble in my hands.

"Okay," I said slowly, a little afraid of what he would ask. "You start."

"What is your favorite color, band, and food?"

"I thought you were supposed to ask one at a time," I said and attached the bauble.

He smirked. "You can ask the next three."

I didn't have to think too hard. The answers were so obvious I'm surprised he didn't already know.

"Pink. Taylor Swift. Sushi." I ignored the fact that he stuck his tongue out at the sushi part. "Your turn."

"Red. The Beatles. My grandpa used to play them around the house, and I still put them on whenever I need some background noise. And you can't beat a good steak."

Jared finished his wreath and held it up for my approval.

Once I gave him the thumbs-up, he added both of ours to the wall of finished wreaths.

My turn.

"What are three interesting facts about you, somewhere you'd like to visit, and an unpopular opinion you have."

Jared burst into laughter and tossed a plastic bauble my way. I tried to catch it, but it bounced off my hands and rattled across the table.

"That's like five questions," he said.

"You asked more than one."

"Yeah, but you made fun of me for just asking three and you ask five?"

I scooted a wreath form in front of him and said, "Go ahead and answer."

He rolled his eyes and started to work on the wreath as he thought. He had attached half the pieces of evergreen when he was finally ready.

"I've been noodling."

"Noodling?"

Jared raised his right hand and pushed back his sweatshirt to reveal his forearm. I noticed that he had a tattoo of a spruce tree on the inside of his arm, perfectly centered between the crook of his elbow and his wrist. It filled most of the space there, but I didn't get long to inspect it. He flipped his hand over and wiggled his fingers.

"Noodling is when you go fishing for catfish, but you use your hands. Your fingers are the bait."

"And they just… bite you?"

"Yup," Jared answered and pushed his sleeve down again, amused by my squeamish reaction. "I met Ryan Gosling in the Denver airport once. I have never broken a bone. I'd like to visit the ocean someday. My unpopular opinion is that I think birthday cake is overrated."

"You've never been to the ocean?" I asked. I felt my cheeks

warm a moment later. Was this another rich kid thing? Did only rich people like my family go stay on the beach every summer? "Birthday cake is one of those traditional things. Like it or not, you get *some* kind of cake on your birthday," I added just to mask my embarrassment.

Jared smiled and shook his head. "Your turn to answer."

I listed off the first few things I thought of. If I thought too long about all the amazing experiences I'd had that set me apart from most people, I would feel embarrassed again.

"I made my own prom dress. I jumped on a shark one time in Cancun. It just swam away, so I didn't see it, but my dad said it wasn't that big. I have a birthmark in the shape of a heart. My unpopular opinion is that coffee is gross."

"And you would like to visit…"

Where would I like to go? I'd been to more countries than I had kept track of. I'd seen so many of the world's great monuments. My family spent every season in a different place when we weren't in school and even then, a few times we finished the semester online.

"Home," I said. I let out a laugh at how stupid it sounded. "My family lives in Heritage City most of the time, but I spent my whole life on the move. I want to be settled somewhere. I'm not as interested in traveling as I used to be. Now, it's just all the hassle of TSA and packing suitcases."

Jared looked a little stunned at first. He'd probably expected me to say Paris. Everyone expected me to say Paris. A smile spread across his face, and he went back to his wreath. I waited for him to take his turn, but he didn't until we'd both finished our second wreaths.

As we worked, I learned that Jared and I had a similar high school experience. We both partied, though the Heritage City Academy parties were a little more involved than the Heritage City High School parties. He told me about the night he nearly got arrested but he and his friends were so big that the officer who nearly stopped them believed that they were college students home for Spring Break and just told them to drive safely.

Like high school, neither of us really partied much anymore in college. He told me it was just like high school 2.0 and he'd paid too much in tuition to spend a school night binge drinking when he had a paper due the next day. I couldn't agree more, only I felt more guilty about having no student loans at all when people around me like Rainy were working overtime every week to save up for the next semester.

"Yours makes twelve," he said and added it to the wall.

The wall was full of pink now, almost more non-traditional wreaths than the usual red and green ones. Jared went to the other side of the room and began pulling on his jacket. He pulled the zipper up to his chin and then fished his car keys from his pocket.

"Ready to hike?"

Ugh.

"This better be an easy hike," I said and followed him out into the snow.

Chapter 11

J ARED DROVE THROUGH C RESCENT P EAK, passing the turn-off for the cabin. He went another mile through the windy mountain road before he turned onto a dirt road that was bumpy with snow.

Was this a sign? Was this a bad sign?

"You said this was an easy hike," I said.

Jared slowed the truck down and pulled off the road where a scenic overlook was. A sign next to the bathroom marked the start of the trail, which led into the dark trees. He turned off the engine and slipped the keys into his pocket.

"The hike won't be as bumpy as the trip here. I swear."

I hopped out and into a muddy puddle. I was glad for the hiking boots now.

It had stopped snowing not long after we'd left the mercantile. The sun was straight above us, and it was almost warm under all the layers we had on. Jared was like an excited puppy just let off the leash. He hopped over the rope separating the parking area from the trailhead and then attempted to ski on his feet, only making it halfway down the hill before he nearly fell.

"Are you showing off?" I asked, picking up the pace to catch up.

He looked back from the sign for the trail, smiling like he had a secret.

"Just being goofy," he said, clearly referencing my comment from our first night out.

Despite the sunlight overhead, it was relatively dark once we started into the trees. The temperature dropped a surprising amount just from the lack of sunlight. For the first ten minutes, all you could hear was the crunch of snow under our feet.

"You said that you didn't like doing winter sports because you like to relax and enjoy the season," Jared said.

"Yes," I answered.

"Is this really not relaxing to you?"

I met his gaze and felt the smile pull at my lips. He was right. This wasn't a hard hike. At least, it wasn't yet. It was more like a stroll through the trees. I felt the most relaxed I had since I'd been home. Somehow, being in the middle of nowhere in the elements was holistic.

"This is perfect," I said, loving the boyish expression that spread across his face.

The trail started to go up the mountain. It was a gentle incline though and after the trees thinned out, I noticed that the snow wasn't as thick. A lot of the trail had melted to reveal the gravel underneath.

"This is so pretty," I said when the trail flatted out. A few feet away, the ground sloped dramatically toward a river. I bet in the summer months people river rafted through here. I wondered if the mountains were still snowcapped then. That was one thing I loved about Colorado, even when winter was over, there was almost always snow somewhere to make my powers tingle. I just never sought out those high places before. Now, looking up at the mountains glittering under the sun, I thought that I might have to do that sometime.

"I think I just changed my answer," I said and pointed at the top of the highest peak. "I think I want to go there."

Jared let out a laugh.

"Give us another forty-five and we can," he said. "I thought we'd save that peak for another time though. The trail up to the top is a bit steep."

"Next time," I said.

"Next time."

We continued walking, a couple of marmots darting across our path and startling me. That gave Jared a good laugh.

"So, your plan after you finish your degree is to come back to the farm and take over?" I asked, trying to distract him from the marmot incident.

"There's so much potential with Crescent Peak, and being between a few big towns and tourist spots. There's also all the traffic from people who come to hike and hunt and such. We could do so much more than just Christmas trees, even in the wintertime."

"I agree. The store could be a cute boutique, which would not only appeal to those tourists, but it would draw people in from those big towns. I'd drive up from Heritage City if McAdams Mercantile sold a cute sweater," I said with a shrug.

"People think of businessmen as these guys in fancy suits in the big city and that's just not my style," Jared said, kicking at a snowbank so the powder rose into the air.

I'd never thought about what working in fashion would look like exactly. It was the same stereotype he mentioned though; big city with expensive people. I'd spent my whole life like that and wasn't impressed by the way most people think of it all. The glamor of it all had dimmed long ago, just like how the college parties didn't excite me after going to so many parties in high school. Maybe it all was old news, but I was beginning to wonder if I was eve really that entranced by it all to begin with or if I was just keeping up with the stereotypes. I used to worry more about having the cool things that made others jealous and being more important than Winnie Maxwell and I'd never thought too much about what I actually enjoyed about it all.

"What happened with you and your ex?"

The air felt icy the moment the words left my lips, and I wondered if I should've kept that thought to myself. Winnie had told me. She said he wasn't involved as much as she was, and it annoyed her. He wasn't that interested in going out to events. I'd called him her boring boyfriend.

"We met at a party during freshman year," Jared said. He started walking up the trail, quickening the pace a bit.

"Like a fraternity party?"

Jared shook his head. "I had enough of that kind of clique in high school. I didn't join one, but I did go to some of their parties. This one was actually a sorority party. My roommate's sister was in the sorority and introduced us— she was Winnie's friend. She introduced us and we hit it off. She recognized me from one of our classes. We started sitting together, exchanging notes, and setting up study dates that turned into coffee dates. A few weeks later she was crashing at our dorm. You know how that goes."

"I don't actually," I said.

He snorted, looking a little surprised. "You haven't dated around?"

"I've dated around, just not since I went away for college."

"Why not? All you'd have to do is walk in a room and say hi to the first guy you saw."

I felt my cheeks heat at the comment. The fact that someone as attractive as Jared McAdams thought I was hot enough to command a room was flattering to say the least. My ego had doubled in size.

"Thank you, but I just don't..." I took a deep breath as it all fell into place. It was all connected. I didn't go to wild parties anymore. I didn't care to jet around the world. I just wanted to be here and do the things that mattered to me with the people that mattered the most.

"You don't have to justify it to me," Jared said. "It makes things less complicated anyway. My ex and I were the same major, so she's in almost all my classes."

I wanted to ask him why he liked her. Why did he still want to be with her when she dumped him over something so shallow? Clearly, she didn't like him that much to begin with.

"So, what happened when you guys broke up?"

He slowed the pace again when we reached the top of the incline. I saw that there was a metal railing at the far edge and a metal bench with a puddle of water in the seat. Jared walked to it and then slowly turned around to face me. He let out a deep sigh.

"She said I wasn't serious enough about the future."

"What?" I asked. The words flew from my lips. Winnie admitted the truth to me. I'd known her long enough to know when she meant what she said. "Was she planning your whole life together already? Did she have a wedding gown picked out?"

Jared shook his head. "Not that. She said I didn't care enough about *my* future. She was super involved in the Future Business Leaders at our school. She was in a sorority. She was doing the whole networking thing I was… I think she's right; I should get a little more involved. Business really is about making connections."

I went after him. I grabbed his elbow and attempted to turn him around. Instead, he just looked over his shoulder at me and gave a weak smile. He shoved his hands deep into his pockets and looked over the railing.

"You don't have to do anything you don't want to. Besides," I said and moved to the railing. The metal was freezing and damp with moisture from the snow. I have an idea.

I raised my hand and took a deep breath, focusing on pulling the moisture from the air until I could feel it pooling in my palm. A little more focus and then a small burst of energy and a solid block of ice sat in my hand in the shape of a Christmas tree. I held it out for him, laughing when I saw the way his eyes lit up.

"Having a successful business is not all about networking and who you know. If you don't have a solid foundation, mission statement, and a good product then you won't have that business for long anyway," I said as he took the ice from me. He turned it over between both palms and then looked up at me in awe. "You have a pretty good thing going with those trees."

"Okay, Elsa. Maybe you got a point there," Jared said and nearly dropped the ice when it slipped from his hand. He managed to catch it against the front of his jacket with the other hand.

"If I'm Elsa in this situation then that makes you Kristoff."

"Is he the one with the reindeer?"

"Have you even seen Frozen?"

"Nope," Jared said. This time, he did drop the ice and it went sliding down the edge of the mountain.

I hadn't realized how high up we were. The river looked more like a stream now. When I looked back up, I was amazed. We were among the peaks. The sun was behind the tallest, sending a kind of moody shadow over our little landing. I noticed the sloped roof of a large building and then recognized the giant deck attached to the back.

"That's the lodge where the Winter Solstice Gala is held," I said and pointed out the building.

"That witchy party you're making me go to?"

I turned to face him, leaning against the railing.

"It's actually a really fun night. I know you aren't excited about getting dressed up in a nice tux, but it's the event of the season for us."

Jared leaned against the railing the way I had so we were face to face now.

"It's the wearing all-white part that has me a little skeptical. You're telling me everyone is wearing white, and no one gets ketchup on their ball gown?"

I laughed and he joined in. We turned back to the spectacular view and watched the sun sink farther behind the tallest peak.

"Admit you liked hiking more than you thought you would," Jared said.

"I already did," I scoffed.

It really had been nice to get outside, and it wasn't like it was anything super sporty. Even now I couldn't imagine how I'd make this competitive.

"I guess we'll have to go find a tuxedo," Jared said under his breath.

I elbowed him. "And dance lessons. There's a ceremonial dance. I'll have to teach it to you."

He groaned and turned from the railing. I followed him back down the slope.

"When do we start?"

"How about we drive to the lodge tomorrow afternoon, and I'll teach you the dance?"

Jared turned around, walking backward just long enough to say, "Make it tomorrow morning. I have to help Mark tomorrow afternoon with a delivery. I'll pick you up at eight?"

He slipped, regaining his footing. He stopped so I could catch up with him, keeping his questioning gaze on me.

"Sound great," I told him. I would have to make sure I was up and ready to dart out the door when I saw him drive up the road. I still wasn't ready to explain all of this to Margot.

I told Jared more about the gala and when the subject of my family came up, I found myself telling him the truth about them. I was honest about how well-off we were, and he didn't even bat an eye. We spent most of the hike down talking about my sisters. I told him some of my favorite childhood stories of both and before we realized it, we were back at the trailhead.

Chapter 12

EVERYONE SLEPT IN EXCEPT MARGOT. I should've known better. We were both up at the same time and met in the kitchen.

"You're up early," she said as she went for the coffee maker. She was dressed in a pair of leggings and a long-sleeve UCLA dry-fit top. A quick glance told me she was on her way downstairs to the gym, not the front lawn. She had on Nikes, not the cleats she'd wear for practice.

"I've been working in town," I said and took a granola bar from the pantry. "It's kind of an internship thing."

"At the mercantile?" Margot asked, a hint of playfulness in her voice.

I ignored it.

"How about you, Marlee, and me go dress shopping in Heritage City this afternoon?"

Margot finished pouring the water into the back of the coffee maker, pressing the button to brew, and leaned back against the counter.

"Sure," she said with a shrug. "I'll ask Marlee."

I took my granola bar and went to the living room to watch out the windows. Margot stayed in the kitchen until she'd finished making a bowl of oatmeal and she had a mug of coffee.

She had just left the room when I saw the silver truck pull down the road.

I grabbed my coat and my purse and hurried toward the door. I was on the front porch before Jared had come to a complete stop in the driveway. Pulling open the passenger door, I hopped in and clicked my seat belt into place.

"Let's go," I said.

"Wow. Eager much?" he teased. He started to back out of the driveway when I noticed a face in one of the upstairs windows.

Marlee.

"I picked up drinks," Jared said, pulling me away from my sister who watched as we drove away. "Hot chocolate with whipped cream and sprinkles."

I picked up the drink, the warm chocolate smell was so inviting that I forgot about Marlee.

"Thanks," I said and took a sip.

The lodge wasn't far from the cabin, just another mile up the road. Unlike the rest of the roads around Crescent Peak, the road up the mountain had been cleared and the pavement was bone dry.

"How did they even get trucks up here?" Jared asked, glancing my way. My expression must've given away the answer because his jaw dropped. "No way. Witches did this?"

"We can't dry the roads, but we can divert the moisture." I showed him. I held a hand over the water that gathered over his side of the windshield and then pulled the beads across until a single pool at formed in the bottom corner of my side. Jared laughed in disbelief.

"What else should I be prepared for?"

"Well, we make the grizzly bear ice statues that are at the front of the building ourselves."

As if on cue, we rounded the mountain, and the front of the lodge came into view. There were two grizzly bears of ice, both standing tall on their back paws, manning either side of the wooden stairs leading to the main entrance.

"To the left," I said as we approached the fork before the lodge. "The right goes to the cabins."

"Are you sure it's fine for me to be here?" Jared asked as he pulled into a parking spot. We were the only car parked in the lot. There might still be people inside who were renting one of the cabins.

"No one will know you're not a warlock unless you tell them," I said and hopped down from the truck.

A few moments later Jared joined me by the headlights, still staring up at the lodge apprehensively. I elbowed him and he relaxed a bit. I led the way toward the building. We took the wooden stairs up to the main doors, which were two massive wooden doors with frosted glass windows. Jared stepped in when I struggled to pull the door open.

The doors opened immediately into the grand ballroom. The marble floors sparkled like fresh snow in the dim light from the giant windows along the back wall. Glass doors opened onto the large balcony, which was where Jared went first.

"This is even bigger than it looks," he said and slid one of the doors aside. I followed him onto the wooden deck. The cool air was invigorating, and I thought for a moment about using my powers to make a snowball and throwing it at him as he looked over the cliffside. I felt a pang in my chest when I remembered why we came here in the first place. Winnie would be at the gala. She would most definitely see us, and I would be in my dramatic, one-of-a-kind ball gown and she would die from jealousy. She'd want Jared back for sure, not that she deserved him. I felt a surprising amount of irritation about that part. Was this worth it?

"So, what kind of dance is this? Waltz? Foxtrot? The hokey pokey?" Jared cabbage-patched back to the doors and I followed him into the ballroom, a little worried about his dancing ability.

"It's a group dance. The elders dance first and then the youngers."

"I'm assuming we're part of the youngers."

I put my hands on both of his shoulders, so he was directly in front of me. Then, I took a step back, putting about four feet between us.

"It goes back to an old folktale about the solstice, the shortest day with the longest night, witches dancing in the night around a fire, etcetera etcetera…" I waved a hand.

"I'm guessing there's no fire thanks to the whole winter witch thing," Jared said.

I ignored the joke. I didn't actually remember the folktale. One of the elders told it at the gala every year before the dancing began. I always showed up afterward.

"The youngers do the exact same dance as the elders. It's supposed to be symbolic."

"The passage of time?" Jared asked.

I shook my head. "The sun and the moon."

"Which part am I playing?"

I pulled my sweatshirt over my head and tossed it aside, adjusting my ponytail. The dance wasn't entirely fast, but the speed built up over time. Jared followed my lead and took off his coat. I was a little distracted for a moment. It was the first time I'd seen him so undressed.

He wore a maroon T-shirt that showed off not only the spruce tattoo on the inside of his right forearm, but his thick biceps too. His black joggers tapered at the ankle, loose enough to be comfortable to dance in yet tight enough that I had to remind myself again the reason for visiting the lodge.

"Okay, so…" I repositioned him again before taking my place opposite him. "You are going to do the same moves I do, just mirrored. Does that make sense?"

"Yeah. I think so," Jared said, that hill starting to form between his brows.

"We'll go slow," I said and started to dance.

Jared was more coordinated than I thought. He caught on quickly and we went through the steps no problem. There were a few moments in the dance where we touched. A brief stroke of the hand, another three-sixty turn with our palms pressed together. I felt the big moment build in my chest and my heart fluttered when it was time for the lift.

With little explanation, Jared lifted me up by my hips and we spun halfway around before he placed me back on my feet. It was so effortless, that rather than let the dance continue to build to the more dramatic moments I stopped and made him rehearse from the beginning again.

The end of the dance was what had me most nervous.

The dance ended with another lift, one that required us to be close. Why hadn't I remembered that part of the dance? This was a bad idea. I knew there was a reason I didn't want to invite him to the gala to begin with. Still, that moment would be the one Winnie would remember forever. The hummingbird my heart was now would be worth that one moment.

I purposely made it awkward. The dance ended with Jared hoisting me into the air and spinning around three times, his hands wrapped just under my butt. His comment from the outdoor store came to mind during the first spin and I spent the next two revolutions attempting to forget about it.

After spinning, he let me slide down his chest. I kept my hands above my head and his rose to meet mine. I turned so my back was pressed to his chest, our hands entwined. Then, I started to walk away, holding on to his hand with my right until the last second.

The room was quiet as we parted and I walked another couple feet away, keeping my eyes on the windows. I stopped and took a deep breath. Damn it. This was a bad idea.

"That's too bad," Jared said.

I turned to look at him, confused by his smirk. "What is?"

"That the sun and the moon can't ever be together," he said. "That's the story, right?"

"Um, yeah." I pulled my phone from my pocket to check the time. It was only ten, too early to use lunch as an excuse.

"I feel pretty good about that. Want to grab some food?"

I crossed the room for my sweatshirt. I pulled it over my head as Jared slipped into his coat.

"I have plans with my sisters today. I think we're going to lunch. I should probably get back and touch base with them."

Jared pulled his keys from his pocket, his expression faltering a little as though not expecting the rejection. He nodded and we started for the entrance.

"So, where do I need to go to get a tux?" Jared held the door open for me.

"I'll look when I'm out with my sisters. We're going dress shopping."

"Okay. Tell me what and where and I'll go get it." Jared's goofy smile made it easier to relax as we got into his truck. Once the radio filled the cab and he started to sing along, everything felt like normal again.

WE TOOK the Jeep into Heritage City after lunch. Marlee was sulking in the back the entire trip— not at the idea of sisterly bonding, but at the idea of dress shopping. I swear, if she could get away with wearing a white sweatshirt and a pair of white sweatpants to the gala, she probably would.

The only formal store in town was also a bridal store, so there were plenty of white dresses to try on. Margot happily looked through the racks on her own. She didn't pick up any of the grander dresses like I wished she would, but at least what she did pick fit the theme.

Margot was deciding between two dresses by the end of our

trip. They were both long. One was sleeveless, with a high neck, and a mesh back. It was simple and wouldn't be high maintenance, as she liked to say every dress that I pointed out was. The second one had long sleeves and a low neckline.

"If you dressed it up with a big headpiece…" I started when Margot came out of the dressing room in the second dress.

"No," she snapped. "I don't want anything that I'll have to keep up with all night. I don't want to spend the night pulling up the top to cover my boobs or making sure my butt isn't hanging out or something."

"They make tape to prevent that kind of thing," I said.

"The first one shows off your muscles," Marlee said, the first time she had participated in any part of our trip. She'd chosen her dress within the first five minutes of being in the store. It was long, a flowy material with loose sleeves that looked a little more like a medieval shift than a gala-worthy gown.

"I think you're right. I like the first better. It covers me a little better." Margot ducked back into the changing room.

I nearly called out that the first dress actually showed off more skin and she wouldn't be able to wear a bra with all that mesh exposing her back. Instead, I looked around the room and stopped when I noticed the small men's section in the corner.

I left Marlee sitting on the plush couch to check the selection. I found a white jacket with black trim along the lapel that I could easily imagine Jared wearing. I knew he didn't like the idea of all white and it was common for the men at the gala to wear black pants, so I pulled a pair from the rack and began piecing a look together. I had just added a black bowtie and was deciding if I should go with a solid black pocket square or one with a little pattern when I noticed that Margot and Marlee had joined me.

"I'm assuming that means you asked him," Margot said.

I turned completely around. I was prepared to deny it, but Marlee didn't roll her eyes at Margot's enthusiasm or say anything about me being boy-obsessed like she used to. She looked intrigued for once as she joined us, her dress draped over her arm.

"Is that who you were with this morning?" she asked.

I nodded. "It's not what you think though."

"She met him at the mercantile on the way to the cabin," Margot said.

Marlee shot me an annoyed look. "That day you made me wait in the car?"

"You said you wanted to wait. You could've come in."

"If you had," Margot interrupted and pointed a finger at Marlee's chest, "then, Madison wouldn't have met Jared."

"Is he a warlock?" Marlee asked.

There it was. The judgement. It crossed her face when I refused to answer.

"It doesn't really matter because it's not what… It's not serious like that." I gave a shrug and took Margot's dress from her with one hand and held another out for Marlee's. She was slow to hand it over, her eyes analyzing me. Marlee could never just accept anything, from a B-grade to anything that came out of my mouth. She had to challenge everything. Ask questions, that was her motto. It should've been anyway.

"If you like him, why not ask him out?" she asked.

I pulled the dress from her hands and started for the register. I was hoping that bringing another set of ears into the mix would keep either of them from rehashing the subject, but I wasn't that lucky.

"Is there another girl? Is he taken?" Margot asked.

I turned from the register after handing the clerk my card. Margot seemed surprised by my forcefulness, but Marlee didn't even flinch.

"I'm not asking him out because we are only here for Christmas and then we both go back to school in different states. So, I have a little crush. He's nice. He's hot. That's pretty much it."

The clerk handed my card back and began to carefully place each dress into garment bags.

"He's your date to the gala though?" Margot asked.

"Seeing the look on Winnie's face when I show up with him is a perk," I said, not willing to mention what kind of "perk" that would be for Jared.

"Can we go home now?" Marlee asked, taking her dress from the clerk. "I have some things to work on."

I contained my jab about her going home to her books or whatever AP homework she wanted to get a head start on. Margot took her dress from the counter, and we went to the Jeep. The conversation moved from boys to Margot's training schedule for the next few days. I didn't even give her a chance to finish inviting me to her morning workouts before I shut that down. I wasn't going to wake up that early.

When we got to the cabin, Marlee went straight upstairs without saying a word. Margot and I hung around the kitchen. I started to make hot chocolate and she scrolled through her phone. I spilled hot water from the kettle over the counter when she gasped.

"What?" I asked. My tone must've been sharp because her smile dimmed a little before she turned her phone. It was opened to her Instagram feed and a post from the UCLA soccer team was front and center. Margot stood in front of the blue and gold background in her uniform with a Santa hat perched on her head.

"They don't feature players in their own post like this unless they're expected to get a good amount of playing time," she said and turned the phone back around. I'd never seen her so excited. Well, maybe not since she got the soccer scholarship to play at UCLA, or maybe that time she scored the goal that won Heritage City Academy the state title.

Either way, instead of making me feel excited about her getting this much closer to achieving her dream of playing professionally, I felt a little sad. I felt distant from her. I didn't keep secrets from Margot, mostly because I was a terrible liar and Margot spent more time around me than Marlee to pry the truth out. I realized as I saw the smile light up her face that I had felt that same kind of feather-light emotion recently. Maybe I had been lying to myself all this time, or at least trying to.

There was one truth I couldn't look past. Jared wanted Winnie.

Chapter 13

I SENT Jared photos of the tux I put together at the formal shop in Heritage City. He invited me to tag along when he went to pick everything up, but I gave him a BS excuse. Normally with the gala just a few days away, I would've been in peak planning mode. I would've tried my dress on and done a test of my hair and makeup. I would've demanded to see Jared in his tux to be sure it fit perfectly. Instead, I was too nervous to focus on the details.

I knew my dress fit exactly the way I wanted because I made it. I also planned out my hair and makeup months ago when I'd made the dress, so there wasn't anything to stress over there. It was seeing Jared in his tux that made me hesitate. I was still messed up from what Margot and Marlee had said when we went dress shopping and I was worried that the minute I saw him looking so dressed up and matching me...

Feeling sad and pathetic annoyed me though, so I only avoided Jared and the mercantile for a day. When I went to McAdams Mercantile, I noticed that the wreath display was full of our pink wreaths with roses and that Jared had added a few new designs. They were impressive. His new design involved weaving together thick pieces of wicker. The bottom left of the wreath had a cluster of white and red baubles with some evergreen pieces stuck throughout, and a big snowflake sitting on top of the design. The top of the wreath had a big buffalo check bow. There was another design he'd made entirely of pinecones with the same buffalo check bow at the top.

"Jared had been sticking new things on the shelves every morning," Mark said.

How did he just appear out of nowhere?

I looked from the wreath display to the rest of the room, trying to find more new additions. "He's more creative than he seems."

Mark snorted. "I think he's learned a thing or two from you. He's talked a lot about business plans and marketing since he started college, but he's never looked at our inventory until you pointed it all out. Our sales are up this year and it's all the changes you two made that are boosting the books."

"Well, your customers will tell you what they want. That's what you should give them, not what is necessarily expected from your business on the grand scale."

"Jared said you want to have your own fashion line when you graduate," Mark said.

I turned from the room to face him. Mark was probably in his early forties. He had the same boyish look that Jared did, the same puppy-like eyes that made it hard not to let him in.

"I'm already working on that," I said and pulled my phone from my pocket. Rainy was the only person I'd ever shown my website to and here I was giving a stranger a personal tour. I showed him the designs I had, all of them listed as out of stock until I was ready to fully commit. I told him about my mission statement, to create trendy designs and make high fashion looks affordable without sacrificing the quality of the clothing. I explained how a lot of brands mark up their items simply because their logos were sewn into the steams or written across the front.

"You should show that to Joanne," Mark said when I put my phone away.

I shrugged. "Maybe another time. Where is Jared anyway?"

Mark pointed toward the back doors of the barn and said, "in the main house. You can go on in. Just make sure you announce yourself."

"Thanks," I said and started for the house. I noticed Joanne near the trees, towing a little sled customers could use if they wanted to cut down their own tree. I waved at her and she gave me a friendly wave back, not concerned that I was on my way to walk into her house.

The house smelled like cinnamon when I walked inside and a quick peek into the kitchen explained why. A couple dozen gingerbread men sat on cooling trays on the counter.

"Jared?" I called out. I stopped at the end of the hallway, not wanting to venture into the more private side of the house.

Jared came out of the back bedroom, a smile spreading on his face.

"You're early," he said and then I noticed the way he moved his right hand behind his back. Was that a box?

"I thought we were meeting in the barn," I said.

He nodded and after a moment of hesitation, he let out a long sigh and held up the box. It was wrapped in red and green plaid paper with a little bow on the top. He walked past me and into the living room, motioning for me to join him.

"I wanted to give you something for doing all of this for me," he said and held the box out to me.

After a moment, I took it. "Jared, you didn't have to. I would've gotten you something if I'd known we were exchanging Christmas gifts."

He shook his head. "It's not for Christmas, it's more a gratitude thing. You didn't have to spend your entire trip home with me and pretending to be…"

"You're right. I didn't have to, but I am."

"Only because I said I'd tell your secret if you didn't."

I put my hands on my hips and sent him the most devious look I could manage. "Like anyone would believe you."

He smirked. "Just open it."

My stomach twisted into all kinds of knots. I pulled the bow off first and then pulled the paper away a little more carefully than I usually would to buy myself some time to prepare. The box underneath was blue with the words *Swarovski* across the top in silver.

No. No. No. He didn't.

"Jared," I said under my breath as I pulled the top off. A dainty silver necklace sat on blue backing. Hanging from the chain was a little snowflake, sparkling with crystals.

"It's really not much," Jared defended as I took the necklace from the box.

It wasn't much by my family's standards, but for him…

"It's more than that it's…" I let out a sigh. As awkward as it was that he wanted to give me a gift like this, I could tell from his face that it made him happy. "Can you help me with it?"

I turned around and held the clasp for the necklace behind me. Jared clasped it and then gently moved my hair out of the way so the snowflake could rest against my chest.

"I was going to say something cheesy about every snowflake being unique just like you, but I thought that part was too much," Jared said with a laugh.

I whirled around to shove his chest at the joke, which only made him laugh more.

"Thank you," I told him, letting my fingers touch the pendant.

"Every snowflake is unique," he said with a smirk. "But they don't all sparkle like you, Madison Sinclair."

"You're so goofy," I laughed.

We stood there for an awkward moment before Jared told me our task for the day. Every year during the week of Christmas, they had a man from Heritage City dress up as Santa and visit children in the barn. Normally, Jared and his mom dressed like elves to help the event go smoothly, but this year Joanne had the bright idea to swap out with me.

"Tell me there aren't pointy shoes," I said as I followed Jared down the hall to retrieve the costumes. I stopped in the doorway of his bedroom. He held up the costume. It was a little green dress with fluff around the hem at the knee. There was a matching Santa hat that was so long that the pom would rest on my shoulder. Unfortunately, there was a pair of pointed shoes that had giant gold bells at the tip.

I groaned when he held it out to me.

"Think of the children," he said with a laugh.

"Was that what the necklace was for, to butter me up before you roped me into this whole thing?" I took the costume from him.

He smiled and joined me in the doorway. "Change in my mom's room across the hall. You think your costume is embarrassing…"

He shut the door before I could look past him for the costume. I went into the room across the hall and shut the door, tossing the elf dress onto the bed. Joanne McAdam's room was half the size of mine back at the cabin. There was a little bathroom attached with a pedestal sink and a round mirror above it that I used to check the way the necklace looked. It was small, but sparkly enough that it made a big impact on my overall look.

I turned from the mirror and reluctantly put on the dress. The velvet was soft, and the dress fit me a little long— Joanne was a few inches taller than me. The shoes weren't as uncomfortable as I thought they'd be, but the tapered end with the bell made them a little clunky to walk in. Not to mention the fact that I jingled with every step. A knock came at the door as I positioned the hat over my curls.

"I'm ready," I said.

The door opened and Jared came in, cheeks turning red behind his wide smile. His costume was the same green velvet. Fluff wrapped around the end of the sleeves and pant legs, which were so tapered that they looked almost like tights. He did a little jig, so his shoes jangled like crazy, the long hat on his head waving back and forth like a ponytail behind him.

Once we both recovered from our laughter, we went back to the barn. The Santa Claus had already arrived and was sitting in a big red plastic chair he must've brought with him. He told Jared and me what he needed, which was for one of us to work the crowd and the other to work with the kids and give out candy canes.

As it turned out, Jared's goofy personality was only brought out more in the presence of kids. He made funny faces to keep the little ones from crying when they sat with Santa, and he always knelt to their height when he gave them their candy canes. It was so endearing that I forgot about how ridiculous we both looked.

That is, until I looked up from the red carpet I was rolling up at the end of the event and saw my mom standing in the entryway.

"Madison?" she asked, adjusting her purse strap on her shoulder. She looked over my elf dress, her confusion growing. "What are you doing?"

"I have been, er, volunteering here," I said. I wasn't getting paid to work at the mercantile, and I wasn't exactly interning either.

"I see. How nice. I'm sure that will look great on your resume," Mom said.

"What are you doing here?" I asked, looking past her. Jared had followed Santa out to his truck with the giant red chair. They'd be back any moment and I wasn't sure how he'd react.

"I heard someone in town talking about all this new stuff in the mercantile and I thought I'd come in."

"Where's Dad?"

My mom shrugged and went back to looking at the display of candles on the front table. "I think he went skiing."

"He actually took a day off from work? Why didn't you go with him?"

"Oh, no. He's out with some work friend," Mom said and lifted a candle to her nose.

"Hey. Can I help with anything?" Jared asked. For a guy so large, he managed to sneak up on us pretty easily.

My mom handed him a couple of candles and picked up a third before I could rescue him.

"Um, Mom, this is Jared. McAdams. His family owns this place." I took a candle from her so poor Jared didn't have to carry anymore. My mom looked from me to Jared, and I saw the change in her expression from casual to professional. It was the way she straightened up even when on the phone with some client.

"Hello," she said and extended a hand to him. "I'm Jennifer Sinclair, Madison's mom."

Jared attempted to stack the candles before deciding to set one down so he could shake her hand properly. The interaction was so formal and stuffy that I caught secondhand embarrassment.

"We should probably finish cleaning up the mess…" I started. Jared shook his head.

"All taken care of. Mrs. Sinclair, Madison told me you're very successful in the world of business. I'm actually studying business at the University of Colorado."

Leave it to Jared to not only meet my mom but try forming a whole relationship with her. If she got involved, then it would only make things more complicated.

My mom finally turned her interest away from her shopping to focus on us.

"I can see why you and Madison would hit it off. You're both interested in entrepreneurship. Do you have any prospects for after graduation? I always have entry-level positions open."

"He already has plans to work for himself, Mom," I interjected before Jared could share too much.

"So, like you," Mom said and gave me a curious look before glancing back at Jared. "I see."

What did she see?

"Jared, I told Mark that I would share some design ideas to expand the clothing area in the mercantile," I said, hoping Mark wouldn't be too surprised when I ambushed him in a few minutes.

Jared nodded and I could tell from his expression that he saw through my excuse.

"It was a pleasure to meet you, Mrs. Sinclair," he said and shook her hand again.

"Madison, be home for dinner tonight. We are going to discuss plans for the gala tomorrow night." My mom was already back to perusing the candles before I could reply.

I practically dragged Jared away from the display, my face burning. He laughed once we'd passed the back doors and were on our way toward the main house.

"She's nice," he said.

"She's busy," I blurted. "All the time."

"Will I meet the rest of your family tomorrow?"

The question caused me to halt on the walkway to the front door. He stopped with his hand on the knob to look back at me.

"Did I say something?" he asked.

I shook my head and joined him. He opened the door, and we went inside, but he didn't go to the hall like I had. When I looked back at him, his expression was concerned.

"Do you not want them to meet me?" he asked.

"It's not that," I said. How did I explain this?

"I know the dating thing is fake, but I thought everything else between us has been very real."

My heart slammed into my chest. I felt like I'd grown roots through the carpet.

"It has been. It *is*. It's just that I'm not a good liar and I worry that I might give it away if we spend too much time with them tomorrow."

Maybe that would do it. Jared seemed to accept it anyway. He relaxed and after talking about how much he wanted out of the pointy shoes, we went to separate rooms to change.

I LEFT the mercantile earlier than normal. Mostly because I wanted to talk with Margot. I set up a nail appointment in Heritage City knowing that I could invite Marlee to be nice and that she would turn me down. It wasn't her thing, just like pretty much anything girly or social wasn't her thing.

So, I went home, picked up Margot after her afternoon practice session in the yard, and we drove back to Heritage City. I chickened out immediately and let the conversation drift to what things were like at UCLA. She was in one of the dedicated athlete's dorms. She told me about all the friends she'd made in her first semester and told me for the thousandth time about how good her chances were of starting in the spring.

It wasn't until we were on our way back to Crescent Peak that the subject of Jared came up and I didn't have to be the one to mention it.

"I'm surprised you picked black nail polish," Margot said as we started up the mountain.

"I thought it tied my dress and Jared's tux together better," I said.

"Speaking of Jared…"

"We're fake dating," I blurted.

The car was silent for a long moment. Only the sound of Mariah Carey filled the car.

"Why? I thought you liked him," Margot finally said.

"I do, but I didn't know… It wasn't supposed to…" I groaned and turned off the radio as Mariah hit a high note.

"You caught feelings after you started fake dating," Margot answered.

I nodded my head and let out a deep breath.

"I don't know if I *really* like him or if I'm just caught up in the whole making her jealous thing and just crushing on him."

"Who are you making jealous? Let's go back to the beginning for a minute," Margot suggested.

We rounded the corner and passed the entrance to McAdam's Mercantile. Jared's silver truck was parked by the utility barn. After a quick scan of the field, I found him pulling a tree on a sled toward the main barn with a couple walking behind it.

"He's Winnie Maxwell's ex. They broke up a while ago and he wants her back," I said.

Margot gasped. "So, you're helping him make Winnie jealous?"

I decided to leave out the part where I accidentally showed him my powers. Even Margot would tell me off for being that stupid.

"I was planning to tell him no. I *did* tell him no and then I got home and was thinking about how he's hot and all the dumb stuff Winnie said at the ice rink. It would only be for the time I was home for Christmas and then we'd go on our way, and I would have the satisfaction of pissing Winnie off and he'd have her back."

"But you like him."

"And he's way too nice. He sees the best in everyone, which is why he can't see how awful Winnie is. He told me about how involved she is at school and in her sorority and that she has all these big dreams, but sometimes people who do good things are bad people. I just don't want him to win her back and then be stuck in some one-sided relationship where he feels like he has to be this other person to be with her."

"And you like him."

I opened my mouth to argue, but I couldn't. I did like Jared. He was totally hot, and I liked him. I liked being with him and he already knew about me being a witch, so that wasn't even the hurdle it usually is for couples.

But he wants Winnie.

"It wouldn't work."

"Why not? How do you know that?"

Did I really have to say it aloud? I glanced her way, hoping it would be enough, but her expression was serious.

"He's in love with Winnie Maxwell," I said. "He even talked about it today."

Margot looked like she wanted to argue. I was glad that she didn't, and she let us drive the rest of the way to the cabin in silence.

Sometimes, loving someone meant letting them do what they felt they needed to do even though you thought they were making a mistake.

Chapter 14

THE NEXT DAY was filled with gala prep. I was the point person for everything hair and makeup related when it came to my sisters. Marlee let me curl her hair, so it hung loose over her shoulders and down the back of her flowy dress. She agreed to letting me do her makeup only if I kept it simple, which I did.

Margot's hair took more time since I decided to do an updo to show off the sheer back of her gown. I spent a long time braiding it into sections that I could fold in at the nape of her neck. It was pinned down so fiercely that it would stay all night — Margot's only request. She let me add a little drama to her eye makeup with a bit of a smoky eye look. As promised, she picked a pair of heels with a strap over the top to wear with her dress.

I was the last one to get ready, which I was glad for since it meant my sisters took the Jeep and our parents had gone early to mingle with the elders. I had the entire quiet house to get ready and deal with all the anxious nerves buzzing through my body.

I wasn't dealing very well.

I took my makeup completely off once after messing up my eye makeup and I had such a hard time deciding what to do with my hair that I ran out of time to do much of anything. I decided to go for a sleek look with my hair and add drama to my face. The gown was the centerpiece here. I didn't want to show it up. I wanted to show off my hard work.

I kept my middle part and pulled my hair into a tight ponytail at the nape of my neck and straightened the ends. I took extra care with my makeup to ensure the smoky eye was even and the lines of my eyeliner were perfect. I dabbed a bit of shimmer in the corners of my eyes and then called it good.

The dress was amazing. I felt the excitement for the night set in as I slipped it on and zipped it into place. The neckline went nearly to my navel, the white sleeves a snug fit on my arms and the bodice sleek to my waistline where it flowed into a large skirt complete with ruffles.

I had picked out my jewelry months ago. I pulled on the sparkly bracelet and put on the large stud earrings but stopped when I went to pick up the matching necklace. It wasn't a perfect match, but I put on the snowflake necklace Jared gave me instead. It was dainty enough that it didn't distract from the neckline I'd worked so long on to get perfect, but it still added a bit of shimmer.

I looked at myself in the mirror for a long time. I felt gorgeous. Not only that, but I felt like I looked exactly the way I wanted the world to see me. I was completely self-made, literally. It was so satisfying to see every angle of that dress that fit every curve of my body as though I'd been born with it on. Every turn was highlighted with a bit of sparkle, as if I was posing for a crowd of people with flashing cameras.

No.

My powers tingled in my veins as a new image came to mind. I was still self-made, completely myself in that dress. Instead of flashing cameras, the shimmer reminded me of walking through the snowy trail in the mountains. My black stilettos could've been a pair of hiking boots as clearly as I remembered the crunch of snow underfoot and the smell of evergreen.

A flash outside my window caught my attention and I saw Jared park in the driveway. I hurried downstairs and to the front door, arriving just as he rang the doorbell. I stopped. So did my heart. I took a deep breath. Everything was going to be amazing. The gala always was, but it would be even better this year. Winnie had already caught me with Jared once, so seeing us together at the gala would be the finishing touch. It would send her over the edge. I couldn't wait to see her face when she saw us dance when she saw us do that finishing move…

I pushed away the memory and answered the door.

He opened his mouth to speak but closed it a second later as his eyes roved over the dress. I ignored the butterflies and focused on his tux. It was the exact white tux with the black trim that I'd picked for him. It looked like he'd bought new shoes to go with the look.

"You look great," I said, feeling my cheeks burn. I was glad to see that he had turned a little pink at the compliment.

"You're beautiful," he said and stepped to the side.

I pulled my coat on and followed him to the truck, accepting his help when he offered to lift me into the seat. It was warm in the truck, almost too warm.

"I'm sorry I was late getting here," Jared said and backed into the road.

"It's okay. I was late getting ready, so you timed it perfectly. They open the gala with the same story every year. So, it's not like we're missing anything big."

The sound of talk radio filled the cab as we drove. I focused on the road as we drove. It was already dark on the mountain as we drove between the peaks. The grizzly bears at the entrance were illuminated by spotlights. Jared took the left into the parking lot, which was so full of cars that it was difficult to find an open parking spot. Amazingly, we found a free spot in the first row near the opposite side of the entrance. Jared parked and instead of getting out, we both sat for a moment.

Jared let out a deep breath and said, "I won't lie. I'm a little nervous."

"Me too," I admitted.

He looked at me and I didn't see an ounce of nerves. He was on the verge of laughing.

"You're a witch. I'm not. Why are you nervous?" He laughed and I couldn't help but smile. It was stupid. He was right. I went to this same gala every year with the same people. It was almost like a family reunion.

"Let's go," I said and hopped down from the seat.

Jared met me at the front of the car, and I wrapped my arm around his in case my heel found a patch of ice across the lot. I could hear the music as we grew closer to the entrance. We'd missed the entire opening ceremony from the sound of it.

Jared pulled open the heavy front door and we walked inside the room of people. It was a sea of white. People of all ages were on the dancefloor moving to the upbeat music. A couple of elders manned the bar in the corner where I found my parents.

"Want to introduce me?" Jared asked in my ear.

Before I could answer the question, my mom noticed us and waved us over. As we walked, she pulled on my dad's arm, so he ended his conversation with a man and turned to look at us. My mom whispered something in his ear, and he reached across the bar for a glass of champagne.

"Mom. Dad," I started as we reached them. "This is Jared McAdams."

Jared reached out and shook my dad's hand.

"Peter Sinclair," Dad said. "Good to meet you."

"My pleasure, sir," Jared said and extended his hand to my mom. She took his hand and gave it a shake. My mom gave me a look of approval before talking to Jared.

"I didn't realize you were a warlock. I would've asked you about the gala had I known," she said.

Jared glanced at me as though asking how he should answer.

"Um, he's not a warlock. No one in his family is."

"How did you two meet?" my dad asked without missing a beat. I was relieved that Jared not being a warlock didn't bother them in the slightest, but how to explain our relationship…

"She was at the mercantile, out by the trees. I love the winter and being outside in it. You could say we found a connection there and then…" Jared glanced my way, a smile pulling across his face. "Turns out we have a lot in common."

"Well, it's good to meet you, son. I promise you we aren't that different from the non-magic folk," Dad said and patted Jared on the shoulder. "Just watch your manners with my daughter. Some dads have shotguns. I can turn you into a popsicle."

"Dad," I moaned as he and Jared both laughed.

"If my mom thought I wasn't being a gentleman then there wouldn't be much left for you to freeze, Mr. Sinclair."

Of course, Jared and his goofball ways had my dad wrapped around his finger. My dad liked his joke so much that he wrapped his whole arm around Jared's shoulders.

"Jared is studying business in Denver," Mom said. "He wants to own his own business."

"I want to take over the mercantile someday, expand the store. Madison has been helping a lot. She's the reason we have all that new stuff in the store right now. It's her eye for design. She's more business-savvy than half the people in my classes." Jared wrapped his right arm around my waist, sandwiching himself for a moment between my dad and me. I knew what my dad was going to say before he opened his mouth. He'd been saying it for years. I was surprised we'd gone this long without hearing it.

"I always told her she should go into business like her mom and I."

"I like designing clothes," I said.

Dad shrugged. "Who's to say you can't do both?"

I guess he was right about that, but still…

"Speaking of fashion, you look very nice, Jared," Mom said and smoothed his pocket square. "I have a feeling that Madison had something to do with that."

"A lot, actually," he replied.

"Marlee! Margot!" My dad waved at both of my sisters, who were talking with some old friends by the windows. When Margot saw me, her eyes lit up. Marlee's mouth formed an O of surprise. They both hurried over to meet Jared.

"This is Jared McAdams," I told them. Margot was already shaking his hand before I could finish introducing them.

"Madison has told us about you," she said.

Oh, Margot.

"Really?" Jared looked curiously at me, the look making my cheeks burn. "Good things, I hope."

"Yes. Not a lot. She just told us that you work at the mercantile and go to school in Denver," Margot said. A quick look at me told me she'd only remembered the girl code after.

"She hasn't talked too much about you two," Jared said.

"I was leaving you guys out on purpose," I added. Jared playfully elbowed me.

"I go to UCLA. I'm on the soccer team," Margot said.

"Cool. What's your major?"

Margot's excitement dimmed a little. She loved to talk about college, her friends, and all the parties she'd been to. She didn't like talking about the actual college part, like anything related to classes.

"I'm still deciding," she said, her smile coming back though not as much as before.

"Marlee is a senior at Heritage City Academy. She's class valedictorian and just got into Yale," I said.

Marlee nodded. She smiled but looked like she was just waiting for the conversation to end so she could vanish into the crowd again.

"You know what you want to study?" Jared asked, probably just to be polite. You didn't come across a girl like Marlee with all her accomplishments, and expect her not to have the next ten years planned out.

"She's going to go to law school," I answered when Marlee didn't.

"Cool," Jared said.

Marlee took that as her cue to leave. She told Jared it was nice to meet him and then was gone. Margot stuck around a while longer to pepper him with questions. They were all things I already knew about Jared or had found out through our game of twenty questions. My dad circled back around when the conversation went to Jared's football days in high school. It was Dad's perfect opportunity to brag about Margot and her changes to start at UCLA. She smiled so much while he talked that I thought her face would freeze that way.

"How old are you, Jared?" Dad asked.

"Twenty," Jared answered.

My dad snapped his fingers and said, "I was going to buy you a beer. Next year?"

"Sure thing," Jared laughed.

"The non-alcoholic drinks are at that table. Help yourself." My dad gave us a wave and we made our way toward a table of punch and canned sodas.

"The punch is always spiked. Usually by the high school kids," I whispered to Jared. He picked up a bottle of water and passed another off to me. I unscrewed the top and before taking a swig, we pressed the plastic bottles together in a toast.

"So, no human sacrifice. No dancing on the graves of our enemies. Pretty lame witch party," Jared teased.

I nudged him with my heel and screwed the lid back on my water.

"Our powers really are as simple as they sound. We are influenced by the seasons. Our powers dim slightly when the season passes. That's why we celebrate now."

Jared downed the last of his water and tossed it into a trash can behind the table. He motioned to the dancefloor.

"Want to dance?"

I did. I wanted to. We would dance. We'd practiced the traditional solstice dance a few times. Besides, you couldn't *not* do the traditional dance at the winter solstice. That's why it was a tradition. But the thought of being that close to him right now… I wasn't prepared yet. I was ready to do the solstice dance, but not… dance.

"I have other ideas," I said and grabbed his hand. I led him past the table and out the glass doors to the deck. The deck was filled with teenagers, some of them high school kids and some of them people our age. It had been the same for the last three years and sure enough, there he was.

"Daren," I greeted.

Daren Krune graduated the same year that I did. We didn't spend a lot of time together, but he was involved in STUCO and was also the one who made most the high school parties happen. Daren looked like he was twenty-one when we were sophomores. So, he was the one who got all the beer at parties and even now, he was stationed on the deck where his stash of beer was carefully placed under hours before.

"Madison, I haven't seen you since graduation night," he said. I tried to ignore the implication of that statement. Graduation night was a blur to say the least.

"Are you still working or are you retired now?" I asked.

Daren gave me a knowing look and then nodded toward the

end of the deck. I led Jared to the railing and as soon as we approached it, a cooler rose to the edge on a growing mound of snow. After I opened the top and pulled out two cans of cheap beer, the mound descended again, and the cooler came to rest on the snow beneath.

"That was amazing," Jared said.

I opened the can with a hiss and then held it out to him. He opened his own and pressed the can against mine.

"Who do you usually come to these parties with?" Jared asked.

Back in high school, most of my friends weren't witches. I usually came with my sisters, and we just hung out with whoever. I had boyfriends, but none I ever imagined introducing to this world. It was weird that not only had I willingly brought Jared into this and told him all about us but that it didn't feel strange at all to do so.

"No one," I said. "I've never had a date before to the gala."

"Are you…?" Jared started, eyebrows raised.

I laughed, stomach twisting. "No. My first time was junior year, and it was terrible."

"Me too. Mine was like pizza though."

"Pizza?"

"You know," Jared said with a shrug. "Hot. Cold. Pizza is always good, not always great though."

I laughed, nearly spitting out my mouthful of beer over the railing. We must've been obnoxious because even the high school kids had moved a little farther away from us. We talked so long that not only had the teenagers moved away from us, but many left the deck entirely.

"It's kinda nice out here in the quiet," I said, looking behind us. There was a group of three girls near the door who were all passing around a pack of gum. They filed back into the building a moment after. Then there was Daren, sipping on a can and staring up at the stars.

"You're not cold?" Jared asked.

I hung my coat on the rack at the entrance. A normal party would have a whole room with attendants to check your coat. Winter witches didn't need that. We could feel the cold air, but it wasn't the numbing sensation that others described. It was invigorating. It was a bit like the way I used to feel after a really good cheer practice. A kind of high.

"No. We can regulate our temperature. I've heard that it's not the same in the heat though," I told him.

Jared smiled and turned his gaze back to the farthest peak. The moon was just behind it, casting a ghostly glow around it. The lights from the parking lot made the snow on the slope of our mountain glimmer under us. I heard an owl hoot in the distance, once, twice, and then I heard another hoot back.

"This is exactly the way I'd like to live after I graduate," Jared said, interrupting the owl's conversation.

It was strange. I'd always assumed I'd be in New York or Paris or working with some designer, but when I thought about all the things I loved about life those places weren't included. I wanted to run my business and expand my shop from online to brick-and-mortar eventually, but I didn't have to be in the fashion capital of the world to do that. I didn't plan on working for any kind of big-name company anyway.

"I've never really thought about it, but I love it here. I always have, but Crescent Peak has always been a vacation spot for me, and you know, vacations are supposed to feel good. I never thought that real life could feel that way too." I glanced his way, and he caught my eye, giving me a smile.

I wasn't sure when it happened, but I realized we were holding hands when he gave mine a gentle squeeze. Maybe now was the time that I brought up how much I liked being around him and how easy it was.

"Madison," Daren called out. "They're calling for the solstice dance now."

Daren tossed his can over the edge of the deck, a swirl of snow guiding it down where the cooler was. I grabbed Jared's can and did the same, not waiting to see that they followed Daren's lead.

My heart thundered against my chest as I led the way inside.

"Elders first," I said, more to calm my nerves. I was a little surprised, but grateful for what happened next.

As the elders formed a circle with their partners, Jared wrapped a hand around my waist.

"We got this."

Chapter 15

THE ELDERS HAD STOPPED MOVING, and all of them paired off. A hush fell over the room. The string quartet at the far side of the room raised their bows. With a wave of the conductor's hands, the music started, and the couples began to rotate. I tried to focus on them the way Jared did. He took a step closer to me, so he was standing just behind me as the dance continued.

I knew every step of the dance, every brief moment of touch between the couples. Everyone in the room did, but I was so aware of those moments that I felt like my body was pulsing. I wanted to indulge in the touch and run away from it all at the same time, but I was frozen in place before Jared.

I held my breath as the music grew quicker and quicker and the couples drew closer and closer. They did more lifts, held hands longer, and lingered with their palms pressed together when they turned. Then, it came time for the final lift, and I reached behind me for Jared's hand as every other younger in the room reached for their own partner.

As the elders finished their lifts and the women and men walked from the dance floor, all the youngers in the room walked onto the floor and took their places. I turned to face Jared, meeting his intense gaze. I wasn't sure if he was just that focused on the dance or if he was feeling the same heart-racing desire that I was.

Before I could decide, the song paused for a moment and then it restarted at its slowest pace. The dance began again.

Jared and I rotated around each other, our right forearms touching once, and then our left arms. We rotated again as the music built in a crescendo. We did the same movements again and then it picked up pace slightly. I kept my eyes on his and I noticed that his expression was different this time as we touched palms instead of forearms.

When the song quickened again, he held on to my hand and spun me around. I kept my arm extended as I followed the couple ahead of us, letting go of his hand at the last second to follow the woman next to me so that were moved in one large circle around our partners in the middle.

When I met Jared again, I knew that what I had seen in his eyes was what I had felt in my chest before. He took my hand in his and pressed the other at the small of my back and we spun twice, close enough that I could smell the spice at his neck. We did the first of our lifts, Jared lifting me by my hips so that I was in the inner circle now.

This time, I stood stationary while he and the other men rotated around us and I was glad when his hands met mine again. He lifted me to the outside again and then he held a hand above my head so I could spin.

The song was at its apex. The deep sound of the cello perfectly contrasted with the sweet melody of the violin over the top. We did our final spin and I turned to face Jared for the last time. His expression was not of the goofy boy I was used to. This was something different.

I walked to him with purpose— one, two, three steps— and then he lifted me into the air above him. I threw my head back toward the ceiling and let my arms extend behind me as he turned in a complete circle. He stopped and I raised my arms above my head, feeling my body slide down his. I was aware of every inch of skin as his torso dragged across mine. Once I'd slid far enough, I stared into his deep expression. I kept my gaze on his dark eyes when I felt my feet meet the floor. Instead of just raising his hands to mine, he let them skim over my hips, my waist, over my ribs, and up my arms.

What I really wanted was to press closer to him, but I turned with the others when his hands reached mine. I started to walk for the glass doors, letting his hand hold on to mine until I was too far away, and he was forced to let go.

I kept walking.

I ignored the applause and kept going, my heart matching the cadence of my steps as I went through the doors to the deck. I turned for the stairs just to the left and started down them, even when I heard Jared call after me. I was at the bottom of the stairs and nearly to the parking lot when I heard the firmness in his voice. It stopped me in my tracks, and made me turn around to face him.

"I haven't thought about her at all tonight," he said, enunciating almost every word. "Not once. I haven't thought about her in days."

I took a few steps in his direction, just enough that I could see his face a little clearer. The moon highlighted his every feature. His dark hair was a stark contrast with his light skin. The black lines on his white tux were perfectly tailored to his muscular body.

"You thought…" he said.

They were the only two words I needed. I closed the distance and threw myself against his hard chest, pulling his lips to mine. His hands gripped my hips, and I felt the pillar of the deck against my back. He lifted me onto the concrete block, and I pulled him closer when I wrapped my legs around him.

His lips were soft against mine, slower than I wanted them to be. I felt like I could rain a blizzard down around us when he slid his hands up my knees and highs, the fabric of my skirt falling around us. His lips moved from mine to my neck and then down to my chest, leaving soft kisses down the neckline of the gown until he stopped with one last kiss where my ribs parted.

"Do you have…?"

"No," I breathed.

I looked down when he didn't speak or move. He smirked up at me.

"Next time," he said and straightened up, cupping the side of my face.

No. No. Maybe we could go somewhere.

He smiled against my lips and said, "Whatever you're doing, you should stop. I think you're freezing my hands to your legs."

I realized now that I was channeling my energy into the places he was touching. Despite wanting to keep him against me, I forced myself to draw my powers in again so he could step back.

"Everyone's inside," I said.

He smiled back at me, drawing in again so his hands were on my hips, holding me in place against the pillar.

"And it's cold out here," Jared said in my ear. He let out a laugh. "It's too cold for me to, um…"

I let out a dramatic groan and he pulled away with a laugh. I thrust my hands out to the side and snow shot up from the ground, soft powder billowing out from both sides of the deck. Jared looked back at me in surprise, a grin spreading on his face.

"If that's what you do when you want me, I'd hate to see what you do when you don't."

"Jared McAdams, will you go out with me, like on a real date this time?"

He gave me one of those playful smiles like he was about to tell me a joke that would have my eyes rolling into the back of my head. Instead, he stepped toward me again and pressed his lips to mine for a quick second.

"I can do you one better," he said with a smirk. "I'll be your *real* boyfriend if you'll have me."

After that comment, I couldn't help myself. I pulled his lips to mine, and I was glad he indulged me. We kissed for a long time and even though I wanted more, I was happy with the feel of his lips on my skin and his strong hands gentle against my waist. We were under the deck until Jared couldn't stand the cold anymore. Then, we moved to his truck.

He was too big to make even kissing in the backseat feasible, so that put an end to the physical side of things. We talked about what our first official date would look like while he warmed up, agreeing to split so that he could plan half the date and I plan the other. It was growing close enough to the end of the gala, so he drove me home and we sat in the driveway talking a while longer.

"I've never met anyone like you," Jared said from the driver's seat.

"I figured that out from the look you gave me when I made that snowman at the mercantile," I said with a giggle.

"No, I really mean that. You're just easy to be around. You're not what I expected."

The last part made my heart sink a little. Not because I was hurt that he thought I'd be some shallow rich girl, but because I used to be exactly that. I used to be the kind of girl who valued being the prettiest, being the most popular, being better than Winnie Maxwell. I couldn't believe I agreed to fake-date him just to piss her off. He deserved more than that.

"My family will be home soon," I said and climbed out of the truck. I heard his window rolling down as I rounded the front of the truck. I stopped and waited for him to speak.

"I felt like I should say something. I don't know what though, something to keep you with me longer," he said and laughed. I went to the window as he leaned out and gave him a kiss.

"As much as I wish I could invite you in, they'll be home soon."

"I know," he said and sat back in his seat. "I think I'm going to like watching you leave about as much as I like watching you walk to me."

I scoffed. "I thought you liked nice round butts."

"I can get over that," Jared said with a wink.

He rolled up the window and started to back out of the driveway.

I SLEPT in the next morning. When I finally woke up, the comforter was wrapped around my legs and my hair was kinked from twisting in the sheets. Sunlight poured through the sheer curtains, which told me it was at least ten.

I pulled my legs free and sat up to check the time on my phone, finding a message from Jared from hours ago waiting for me.

Last night was fun. I can't wait to see what a real date with you looks like.

I WENT to type my reply but stopped. I couldn't explain the electricity I felt at the thought of another date. I was going to see him later today anyway. I sat my phone down and went to the bathroom.

The hot water was almost as nice as being wrapped in the bedsheets. I stayed under the spray even after I'd finished washing my hair and body. I dried my hair and pulled it into a French braid down my back. I picked a comfortable, but cute outfit. My pink leggings with the jean jacket and white sweater, pairing them with my black, heeled boots. I finished my makeup and then pulled on Jared's hat before going to my bed to grab my phone.

I noticed the missed call first. Jared. Then, I saw all the texts and felt the creep of anxiety.

Got a minute for a call?

I just wanted to let you know that I won't be free today.

I swear I'm not blowing you off after our night. I definitely want to see more of you.

I didn't mean that to sound that way. I mean that I want to go out with you again soon.

I'll call you when I get back.

I COULD PRACTICALLY HEAR the way he would laugh after his dirty joke. It settled my nerves a little. I believed him. Mark had been talking this week about doing a pop-up shop at a Christmas parade a few hours away. Tomorrow was Christmas Eve, which was hard to believe, and I needed to finish shopping anyway. I had the book and jewelry for Marlee, but I wanted to get something more for Margot and after going to the outdoor shop with Jared, I was sure I could find something there.

I opened the messaging app and texted my response.

· · ·

I DIDN'T HAVE to wait long for his reply.

I BIT DOWN on my bottom lip. Joanne was tough as nails, but something about her warmed my heart. She was a true mama bear and I felt lucky to feel included as one of her cubs. I sent Jared the text agreeing to meet him tomorrow afternoon and slowly made my way downstairs. Pouring myself a bowl of cereal, I was in such a daze that I didn't see Marlee and Margot sitting in the living room until I turned from the kitchen counter and noticed them staring.

"You kinda disappeared last night," Margot said and sipped on her mug.

I felt my cheeks flush. "I was there."

"Not for long," Marlee laughed. "You left your coat."

I forgot about having one last night. It wasn't like I really needed it to keep warm. I took my bowl of cereal and went to the opposite side of the couch from Margot.

"Where are Mom and Dad?" I asked.

"You know they're working. You aren't going to change the subject that easily," Margot told me and tucked her legs under her, turning to face me.

I let the excitement bubble over, and my cereal went mushy by the time I gave them all the details. I told them how romantic the dance was and how we kissed under the deck in the snow. Marlee looked more and more uncomfortable as I talked about the feeling of Jared against me, so I stopped talking and let Margot ask her questions.

No, we didn't do it.

Yes, we were boyfriend and girlfriend.

Yes, we were planning to spend tomorrow together.

"It's funny," Marlee said and sat her coffee on the side table. "This is the least boy-crazy I've ever seen you. Normally, you would've told us about how hot this guy is the day you met him, and you've hardly mentioned him at all. You have, but not in that obsessive way."

She was right. I think most of us are caught up in how our crush looks way before we ever know who they really are. That's how I usually did things. Date the hot guy, show up places on his arm like a curated pair, then realize things weren't clicking the entire time and we break up.

That's not what I liked so much about Jared. His tight body was a huge perk though.

"He's just a really nice guy. It's the best part about who he is. It's so easy to talk to him and he doesn't make me feel like some cute, little girl the way other guys make me feel. I feel like I stand just as tall as he does," I said. I scoffed at the thought of my five-five frame next to his six-five stance.

"I think he's nice," Margot offered.

"Me too," Marlee said.

That caught our attention. Marlee was a good judge of character, like really good. Her analytical mind saw right through all things bullshit and if she not only couldn't find anything wrong with Jared but actually liked him… I felt like my heart would swell right out of my chest.

"I have to go run an errand in town, but we should all do something this afternoon," I said and got up from the couch with my mushy cereal in hand.

"I'll go with you. I want to check out the market for that good coffee from Telluride," Margot said.

"No." The words fell from my lips, so fast that I couldn't recover from the suspicion on my sister's face.

"You're Christmas shopping, aren't you?" Margot asked.

Marlee looked up from her book to point out, "Tomorrow is Christmas Eve, and everything will shut down."

Thanks for stating the obvious.

"Cut me some slack. I've been a little busy," I said and sat the bowl in the sink.

"I'll say," Marlee scoffed as I pulled my keys from my purse.

I decided to let the comment slide and went to the garage. One day, Marlee would leave the nest and learn something she didn't expect about herself that would make her more bearable to be around. At least, we could hope.

Chapter 16

I ENDED up getting Margot a pink sweatshirt, which would probably be one of the few items in her college closet that wasn't blue and gold. I didn't think about how little she'd actually get to wear the fleece-lined sweatshirt since she lived in California now. It was still adorable, and it matched the pants and cute sneakers I bought for her. A complete outfit.

I wrapped all the gifts for my family late that night and snuck downstairs to put them under the tree near midnight. I would've slept in again except Marlee woke me up by pounding against the door.

"Dad's making waffles. He wants us all together for breakfast," she called.

I groaned and after hearing Mom call down the hallway a little later, I gave up on straightening my hair and pulled it into a ponytail. The rest of my outfit was cute though, festive even. I wore jeans and my favorite red sweater, the snowflake pendant sparkling over my chest.

"Morning. You've been sleeping a lot lately," Dad said and flipped a waffle onto a plate.

I took a seat on the remaining barstool next to Mom. She rubbed my back and took the plate from Dad, setting it in front of me.

"She's been out late with Jared," Margot said as though everyone should've seen it.

"Not out late," I said and sprayed a dollop of whipped cream onto my waffle. "We've just been spending time around the mercantile. I wasn't lying when I said I was kind of interning there."

"Paid or unpaid?" Dad asked. It didn't really matter. He'd have an opinion either way.

"More like volunteering," I said under my breath, glad when Marlee asked him to pass her the maple syrup.

The kitchen was quiet for a moment while we all ate breakfast, growing into the usual awkward silence no one knew how to interrupt judging by the way we glanced at each other in hopes that someone would attempt to free us. Today, that person was Marlee.

"Mom, can you help me with my paper for my AP Lang class?"

"What's it about?" she asked.

Marlee droned on and on about her essay about some subject— I completely tuned out before she could fully explain it. All I knew was it was something that Mom *and* Dad had a lot of experience with at work and the snide comments came left and right as they did that thing where they paid each other really nice compliments that actually were just backhanded comments.

Maybe I would get to straighten my hair after all.

"I have to get ready. I'm helping at the mercantile," I said and hopped down from the stool. It put an end to the bickering as they all looked at me in surprise.

"On Christmas Eve?" Mom asked.

"You'd think a family-run business would take the holidays off," Marlee muttered.

Dad scoffed. "I think it's a testament to their entrepreneurial spirit. Do the work you have to to set your business apart."

Now, I really had to get out of there.

"They're just wrapping up, so I'll be back early," I said on the way upstairs.

I straightened my hair like I wanted to and wrapped the last present. I stalled for a long time, running through all the reactions the gift might get before I decided it was long past time to go. I tucked the gift in my purse and left for the mercantile.

The parking lot was empty. Jared's silver truck, Joanne's Explorer, and Mark's truck sat on the gravel roundabout in front of the little blue house. It had started to snow, thick flakes falling across my windshield, as I sat with the engine idling and deciding if I should park at the house instead.

I was startled when the passenger door opened.

"Sorry," Jared said with a laugh as he climbed into the Jeep. "I was locking up the barn."

"I kinda went on autopilot," I said as he clicked his seat belt into place. "I didn't think about us meeting at the house."

"That's okay," he said with a boyish smirk. "Buys us a little time for this."

He leaned in, a hand slinking over my cheek. His lips moved slowly, gentle on mine. I wasn't sure how long we kissed, but it wasn't long enough. He pulled away and laughed.

"I love your mom, but would she really miss us?" I asked, joining his laughter.

"She made lunch," he replied. "Most days she tosses me the bread and tells me to find something in the pantry to make a sandwich."

I laughed and put the Jeep in drive. I drove around the property to the little gravel road that led to the blue house. I could see the Christmas tree glittering in the living room window. Jared led the way inside, both of us leaving our wet shoes by the door on the way to the kitchen.

Mark was excited to see us and from the smell of him when he pulled me into a hug, maybe a little buzzed. After, Jared whispered in my ear that Christmas Eve had specific traditions at the McAdams house. Mark must've overheard him, because he launched into the long explanation, telling me about the time his and Joanne's dad tried deep-frying a turkey at Thanksgiving and nearly burning the garage down. He was so embarrassed that he was determined to master the culinary art and tried again at Christmas, which proved almost just as disastrous.

"This time it was the lawn that got the brunt of it," Mark said through his laughter. "There's used to be a spruce out front."

"Mom got drunk on wine. She'd spent the day making a backup turkey, but she fell asleep on the couch before she could enjoy any of it, and Mark, Dad, and I ate at the table while Dad tried figuring out how to deep-fry a turkey for next time," Joanne said with a laugh.

"Now, every Christmas, Joanne fries a turkey and I get drunk," Mark joked. We all laughed. Mark told more stories about their family while Joanne finished carving the turkey and I tossed the spinach salad. We sat around the kitchen table, taking turns telling our favorite family stories and eating way too much turkey and stuffing.

We went around the table until I was out of stories, which happened pretty fast. Most of my stories were about my sisters. I had a few about Dad. A lot of my childhood memories were a dream to most— the beach, skiing, and visiting other countries — but to me all that stood out was my parent's bickering or their constant leaving events to take calls.

Jared found a board game in the closet, and we played until Mark won, celebrating by throwing his hands into the air and knocking his beer onto the board. We scrambled to clean it up while he apologized over and over. Jared nudged my arm when Joanne took the sopping napkins to the kitchen and Mark moved the board to the counter to dry.

"Want to escape to the barn?" he whispered.

"Yes." I stood up before he could say anymore.

"Madison has to get back to celebrate with her family," Jared explained when Mark and Joanne looked up from the kitchen counter.

"Thank you for having me over. Lunch was amazing and you guys have been... amazing." I felt the blush creeping over my face.

Joanne came around the counter to give me a hug and wish me a merry Christmas. Mark wrapped an arm around my shoulders and gave me a squeeze, telling me not to let his knucklehead of a nephew give me too much grief. I followed Jared back to the front lawn and we got into the Jeep. I drove back around to the barn and parked at the front of the lot.

Jared pushed the door aside, the metal letting out an ear-splitting squeal.

"Sorry," he said and gave it one more noisy push so it opened all the way. "I'll get the lights."

I didn't wait for him to light the room before I walked inside. I could see the shapes of the tables, the single circular rack of clothes, and the register counter. I stopped to inspect the cards sitting there. The lights flicked on, and I was able to inspect them closer, scanning local business after local business before I heard someone running behind me.

Before I could turn, a pair of arms wrapped around my waist. My shriek turned to a giggle as Jared held me tight and pressed soft kisses along my neck. I managed to twist around to face him. He lifted me onto the counter and stood between my knees. Now, he was the perfect height to kiss him, the kiss growing deeper and deeper until he pulled back.

"Hold that thought a moment," he said with a smirk. He leaned over the counter, tall enough that he could reach into the shelf behind it. He straightened up with yet another little box wrapped with buffalo plaid.

"What could this be?" I said playfully and took the box. He waited while I pulled the paper off. It was another Swarovski box. Inside were a pair of snowflake earrings to match my necklace.

"After the gala, I thought you deserved a complete set." Jared kissed me when I wrapped my arms around his neck. I hopped down from the counter and reached for my bag. I pulled out the gift I'd gotten for him, a rectangular box wrapped in red wrapping paper and topped with a burlap bow.

"I got you something too," I said and handed the gift to me.

He smiled and ripped off the paper. The brown box was stamped on top with the name of the custom craft shop. Jared paused before he pulled off the lid. He took out the pocketknife first. McAdams was engraved across the thick wooden handle and the logo I created was engraved at the bottom. Jared admired it in awe for a long moment before he looked down at the box. There was also a leather bracelet that had a tree stamped into it to match the one tattooed on his forearm. I wanted to do more with the logo, but the seller suggested that she put it on a blank business card with the shop's information. That way, the McAdams could walk in and have her put the logo on anything they wanted.

"This is amazing. You got this downtown?" he asked, finally looking at the logo on the business card. It was the outline of the big red barn with the tops of evergreen trees peeking out from behind the roof. McAdams Mercantile was written under the barn in a pretty font.

"The owner of the shop told me you could bring that card in, and he could use the original file he has to put that logo on anything. He can engrave, do T-shirts, and he even has this huge laser printer that he showed off twice to me. He said you might have to bring or ship to him the items you want him to do, but I thought it was cool. You guys really need your own logo."

Jared pulled me into a hug. I heard him set the gift on the counter behind me, the knife rattling as it settled into place.

When he pulled from the hug, he took my face between his hands and kissed me.

"It's like we've been missing you all along," he said.

My cheeks flamed. I loved fashion and designing, but I think I liked discussing the business side of things with him more. It was fun to do that kind of planning and meeting the wants of the customers, like making all those pink wreaths was more satisfying than getting an A on my gala dress project. It kind of made me wonder if I really needed the fashion side of things to be successful. I was planning to launch a clothing business, after all. I wasn't planning to sign up to work for Chanel or anything. That sounded miserable.

"When I'm with you..." I stepped away from him. If he kept looking at me with those puppy eyes, then I'd never say what I wanted to. "I don't feel like one of the Sinclair sisters. I don't feel like some trust-fund baby or spoiled girl, even though I am. I know I am. You make me feel like I'm just Madison."

"You are just Madison," Jared said so simply that it made me laugh. He smiled and kissed me on the forehead. We wandered around the barn for a while, talking about the different ways we could offer more branded products now that there was a logo for McAdams Mercantile and the different kinds of clothing that should be added to that section of the store. It wasn't until I started telling him about a few ideas for cute sweaters that I realized we were talking about the store like it was ours.

"You're probably right about at least selling branded T-shirts. I bet we can get a good deal on them with a seller in town," Jared said as we went outside. The flakes were huge now, an inch deep by the look of the drifts around the Jeep's tires.

"That's what the owner of the custom craft store told me. Don't go cheap with the shirts though. Get something soft. That's a selling point when it comes to those kinds of touristy things," I said as he locked up. Jared walked me back to the Jeep.

He kissed me before shutting my door and then I headed back into Crescent Peak.

Thankfully, things were calm at the cabin. Our Christmas Eve consisted of a family dinner where no one argued. It was actually nice. We talked about our plans going into the new year. Marlee told us about all the things left on her college enrollment checklist. She was most nervous about picking a roommate. Honestly, I'm sure any roommate at an Ivy League school would be a good match for her.

Margot was excited to move into spring training and prove herself worthy of a starting spot. Margot and Dad talked about it for so long about it that the rest of us left them at the table and went to set up for our movie night in the living room. *The Polar Express*. It was a family Christmas tradition to watch *The Polar Express* on Christmas Eve and drink hot chocolate before bed.

Once the movie ended, Mom and Dad were more than ready for bed. Dad had fallen asleep near the end of the movie and was a little upset that no one woke him up. They went to bed ahead of us. Margot cleaned up the popcorn. She always was the responsible one.

"I'm going to bed," Marlee declared. "No present shaking!"

I almost made a joke about her getting everyone books as presents, but I caught myself. It's Christmas Eve. No one argued. Mom and Dad didn't even talk about work all evening. *Don't ruin the magic of the season.*

"Pinky promise," I said and held up my little finger for her to see. Margot did the same. If we were a couple of years younger, we would've investigated the presents to try to figure out what we were getting. Marlee hated surprises. One of my favorite memories was the time my mom thought it would be fun to throw a surprise birthday party for my youngest sister and she burst into tears at the room full of people. I was convinced that Marlee already knew what all her presents were. That Ivy

League brain came in handy sometimes and I was sure she did all her snooping before the gifts ever went under the tree.

So, who was she to scold us?

"What did you get her?" I asked Margot.

She let out a long sigh as though whatever it was wasn't good enough.

"I got her a few of those clothbound classic books for her collection."

"I never understood why she didn't just buy the whole set."

"She says she has to read them first. She doesn't like to have unread books on her shelf," Margot said with a giggle. "What did you get her?"

"A book," I laughed before adding, "and a couple of necklaces. They're cute."

We finished cleaning up the living room and Margot started the dishwasher. Despite wanting to, neither of us even touched the gifts under the tree before heading upstairs.

Chapter 17

CHRISTMAS DAY MADE me feel like a kid again. The entire family was up earlier than normal to exchange gifts and enjoy homemade breakfast. I was in charge of preparing all the ingredients for omelets, which was fine with me because I was a terrible cook. Margot made the omelets, Marlee prepped the table, and Mom and Dad made themselves mimosas and sorted the gifts under the tree into piles. Once breakfast was made, we ate in the living room while taking turns opening gifts.

Margot went first. She loved the casual outfit I put together for her. Marlee gave her a memoir by some famous soccer player. Mom and Dad bought her several new outfits, a new laptop, and the newest iPhone.

Marlee was surprised by the book I got her but masked her disappointment well. She did like the necklaces though, and mentioned a sweater she thought it would look good with. Mom and Dad gave her the same gift they'd given Margot but in more of a Marlee style. Instead of athleisure, they had gifted her cozy sweaters and oversized cardigans. Margot gave her some Yale-themed presents, like a stuffed animal of a bulldog wearing a Yale sweater. She also gave her a few of those clothbound classic books she loved so much. Why anyone would willingly read *Moby Dick*, I would never understand.

Mom and Dad were happy to receive our gifts. At least, that's what they kept telling us. It felt a little like the way you tell a kid their drawing is so good. It's always nice to get a gift, but when you could literally buy the stock in a Versace store, gifts didn't carry the same punch. My sisters and I had learned that giving them gag gifts brought more joy to the holiday than trying to find something they actually wanted. So, Mom happily accepted her cheesy T-shirt, Boss Bitch coffee mug, and an assortment of office supplies with snarky sayings printed on them. Dad found the apron Margot got him to be hilarious. I bought him a new set of grilling utensils and Marlee bought him a couple of different cookbooks that kept him entertained while I started to unwrap my own gifts.

Of course, Marlee got me a book. Thankfully, it wasn't some stuffy classic or dense nonfiction book. She got me a romance with a cute couple holding hands on the cover. Margot gave me some jewelry. Mom and Dad, though I knew it was really Mom, always gave me the best Christmas gift. I got a new purse and a couple of dresses that I couldn't wait to wear.

We spent some time admiring our gifts and doing a try-on of the clothes Mom and Dad gave us. It was a family tradition that my sisters slowly grew out of but walking down our pretend catwalk was fun to me even now. Marlee was never was really into it and had stopped participating when she was about fourteen. Once she'd graduated high school, Margot thought she was too grown up to let loose and have a little fun. So, this year it was just me trying on the outfits for Mom, the only person who seemed interested in seeing how they all came together.

"I can't wait until one of you brings a boy home for Christmas," Mom said while sipping on her second mimosa. I noticed how her eyes lingered on me.

Dad scoffed. "You all have better things to focus on. I have my entrepreneur," he said and winked at me. "Superstar here is going straight into the pros after she graduates." Dad pulled

Margot into a tight one-armed hug before pointing to Marlee and saying, "And my little bookworm is going to make waves in the courtroom. The boys will come to you. Don't worry about finding them yourselves."

Mom rolled her eyes and took a drink, but when Dad raised his glass to her in a toast, I was glad to see her smile and press her glass to his with a clink. They didn't once mention work or even look at their phones the entire day. It was well into the evening before any mention of the next workday even came up. Even then, they were both planning to sleep in a few hours longer before checking their emails and jumping onto Zoom calls.

We played board games and watched more Christmas movies. Margot took the day off from training and we had a snowball fight in the backyard. We used our magic, of course, to conjure snowballs and fire them at each other. Margot was quick enough on her feet to dodge and Marlee was smart enough to use her powers to create a barricade between us and her wherever she was. I wasn't so lucky.

Marlee won. I don't think anyone would've bet against her though.

"What did Jared get you for Christmas?" Marlee asked. I was a little surprised that she seemed genuinely curious. Margot's expression mirrored that.

"He got me earrings to match the necklace he gave me a few days ago," I told her, moving my curls away from my face to show off the studs. They both admired them for a moment, commenting about how well they went with the necklace and how pretty they were. I loved them and not just because they were from Jared. The earrings and necklace were my favorite accessories, including the diamond earrings, I got for Christmas last year from Mom and Dad.

"He seems really nice," Marlee said. That meant a lot coming from her and I met Margot's surprised expression.

"He is. He's the only guy who's never seen me as… well, as a Sinclair," I said.

They both seemed to understand that. It might have been the one thing we all had in common. I was thankful for everything our parents gave me. I didn't have any student loans. I had name-brand clothes, a new iPhone each time a new version came out, and a ticket to wherever our parents were planning to vacation at least twice a year. It was hard to complain when you had all of that, and none of us ever did, but still…

Honestly, as much as I complained about her, Marlee had the best analysis. A few years ago, she said that she would never have enough books. No matter how many she read or how many she collected on her shelf, there would always be more out there and more that she wanted to read. She said that our parents were a little like that. They could give us everything we wanted and still wouldn't have enough.

For me, it was their approval. When I mentioned my business idea to Mom, she thought I was missing out on a big opportunity. I was at a great fashion school. I had a huge amount of talent as a designer. Our family name carried enough weight to catch the attention of some high-level people in the industry. She thought my eyes should be set on working my way up in the ranks of high-fashion designers. She even took me to New York Fashion Week to show me what was out there But I still wanted to explore the idea of making high fashion for everyone.

"Have you met his family?" Margot asked.

I told them all about Joanne and Mark and what I knew about their parents. They were just as fascinated by Jared's high school days as I was, and they listened to me retell a few of his childhood stories.

"You really love him, don't you?" Margot asked.

I opened my mouth to agree, but the L-word caught my attention. I'd dated many guys. I told a few of them that I loved them, and I thought I had but this was different. This felt easy and deeper somehow. Was this what love *really* felt like?

"Maybe," I said with a shrug.

"I think he's nice," Marlee said. She was beginning to sound like a broken record. Marlee rarely displayed deep emotions, so I was sure she meant it this time. If Marlee thought Jared was a great guy and she approved of him as my boyfriend, then that meant a lot.

It snowed tons that afternoon, so we stayed inside and played Monopoly. I remembered near the end why I never played this game. Marlee and I got too competitive. I could see the judgment creep into her eyes near the end of the game and I used Jared's text as an excuse to forfeit.

"You know that means I win," Marlee called after me as I moved from the dining room to the living room chair by the window. It had snowed so much that the road was covered in white, and it was hard to tell where our yard stopped and the road to Crescent City began.

Merry Christmas!

Merry Christmas to you too! Tell Mark and your mom I said hi.

They told me to tell you hello. I showed them the logo you made, and they love it. Mom already added it to our website.

I OPENED the browser on my phone and typed in McAdams Mercantile. Just like he said, a website address came up. It was a single page with a photo of the entire McAdams family, Jared's grandparents included, standing in front of that famous red barn. Their mission statement was listed in a single paragraph underneath. It looked good. It was professional and sleek. It was exciting and made me happy to see the possibilities Jared and I had discussed becoming reality. He wanted to expand the family business and here he was, taking the first step.

When I looked up, Marlee was thumbing through the book I got her. I watched as she slowly flipped the pages until she made it to the back cover. She looked at the front cover and then flipped to the first chapter and began to read.

Maybe she wasn't that much of a stuffy brainiac after all.

I went upstairs for my laptop. I spent most of the afternoon working on my own website and designs. Marlee read through a good chunk of the book while we sat. When she finally looked up from the book our eyes met.

"This is pretty good," she told me and held up the book.

"You're welcome," I said. "Maybe I could borrow it when you're done, and we could talk about it?"

She shrugged. "Sure."

Finally, a connection.

THE DAYS after Christmas were slow at the mercantile. I sensed the McAdams's discouragement when I arrived the first day. We marked down the Christmas wreath prices, but thanks to our new designs many of them stayed at full price and were nearly as popular as before. It was the only thing keeping Mark and Joanne's spirits up. Jared seemed more distracted than usual, but I ignored it for the first couple of days. It was probably that our time off from school was coming to an end and we would have to do the long-distance thing. I was feeling the same pit in my stomach when I thought about it.

It wasn't until he kept a straight face when he tripped over a branch down one of the rows of trees that I knew something was wrong.

"You've been different the last week. Did something happen?"

Jared shrugged. "Hmm. I'm just same-old-same-old."

"Was it something I did?"

Jared dropped the rope to the sled he was towing and stepped in front of me.

"No. You didn't do anything. It's nothing to do with you," he assured me. He put his hands on my shoulders and brushed my curls from my face.

"What's on your mind?" I asked and pulled him closer by the pockets of his jacket.

He opened his mouth to speak, but no sound came out. He let out a deep breath and said the words that I'd worried about for weeks.

"I talked to my ex."

My heart thumped hard in my chest. I hadn't seen Winnie in weeks, not since the diner. Jared and I had spent so little time at the gala that I forgot about Winnie even being there. We spent most of our short time there on the deck, so unless she saw us during the dance…

"Oh. Okay," I said slowly.

"I never realized…"

Oh no. I should've just told him I knew her. Making her jealous was what we both wanted, so I didn't even think I needed to explain myself. Did it really matter?

"I'm sorry," I blurted.

Jared snorted and looked down at me with an amused smirk. "*You're* sorry? Why? I should never have asked you to pretend in the first place. After spending some time apart from her and meeting you… You're the complete opposite of her and I never even realized it. I didn't see how stuck-up she was. I do now. Wow, that girl thinks she's entitled to a lot more than most."

I laughed, the sound a little awkward. Jared didn't seem to notice as he laughed too. I was glad that he found it so funny. It made me relax a little.

"It's funny how sometimes it takes time away from the things we want so much for us to realize that maybe we didn't really want them to begin with," I said. The words stuck in my head. For a second, I wondered if I'd even said it out loud. Maybe Jared was the one who spoke, but the curious look he gave me told me I had.

"What do you mean?" he asked.

Good question.

"I haven't thought about my fashion classes all this time," I said after a moment.

It didn't register to him how big this was. I spent all my teen years imagining my designs on a runway of models and in shops around the world. That's always the image I had and even now, that's the way I imagined my work being represented. But that's not what I was doing. None of my actions supported that vision and I was okay with that. Maybe the vision was wrong. What if I was imagining what I thought that should look like through the expensive lens of my family and not my own?

"You should join the business world," Jared said and bent over to pick up the rope to his sled. "You'd be good at it."

"Yeah. I think so too," I said and fell into step beside him.

Chapter 18

JARED and I negotiated who would get to pick out the next date. When neither of us gave in to the other, we agreed to split. Jared would plan the afternoon on New Year's Eve, and I would get to pick the evening. The only agreement was that whatever we did had to be in Heritage City.

We'd gone on several hikes and explored every store in Crescent Peak to the point that the shopkeepers knew our names. We needed to get out.

"Will you at least tell me what we're doing tomorrow?" I asked as Jared walked me to the Jeep in the parking lot of the mercantile.

He laughed and said, "No. That's the whole point of a surprise."

"Jared, I'm just asking so I can plan my outfit," I said, moving to the side to avoid a threatening hand from tickling my side. I bumped into the fender of the Jeep, and he pinned me there, stopping closer so my only hope was to squeeze past his arms on either side of me. I was frozen in place, practically melting under his wry smile despite the thirty-degree temperature.

"It was your idea, Elsa," he joked.

I put my hands on his chest to give him a playful push but

stopped short. Ugh. Why did he have to be so hot? I felt the warmth flood my face.

"Let me guess. Jared McAdams wants to do something outdoorsy for our New Year's date. I should wear active wear and sensible shoes," I said and let my hands fist around the fabric of the shirt under his jacket.

He smiled and said, "And something tells me I should wear a tie and pinchy shoes. Madison Sinclair has expensive taste."

I pulled him closer, rising onto my toes so my lips could find his. He didn't move his hands from the Jeep behind me, which was frustrating. Before I could do anything about it he pulled away with an onery look on his face.

"Wear the activewear. Pack your dress," he said and lowered his arms.

"Don't forget your pinchy shoes," I teased as he opened the driver's door. I climbed in and he shut the door behind me.

The drive was so short to the cabin that I didn't bother connecting my phone to play any music. I settled for the radio instead. The entire drive up the mountain to Crescent Peak was filled with a weatherman reporting on heavy snowfall expected next week and how to prepare and keep warm in case we were stuck at home. I wasn't quite ready to go home yet, so I pulled into a parking spot across from the coffee shop as the radio hosts debated the best way to stay sane while snowed in.

I noticed the man with his guitar first as he set up in the front window for his set. It wasn't until I crossed the street that I realized how busy it was. I went inside and ordered my hot chocolate without needing to wait in line. All the people were gathered at the tables around the singer who was playing an upbeat song.

"He brought in a good crowd," I said to the barista as she handed over my debit card.

"Oh. They're here celebrating that tall guy," the woman said and pointed to a boy sitting at the table in the middle of the group. I recognized many of the faces now; a lot of them were people I went to high school with. I noticed Winnie and her sorority sisters at the tables nearest me and hoped she didn't look up and see me.

"That guy set a college swimming record before Christmas," the barista said.

"Wow," I said a little absentmindedly. I was still worried about Winnie noticing me, but I tried to ignore her. The boy was laughing with his friends. I noticed Daren Krune to his right. They looked a lot alike. Didn't Daren have a little brother? He did. He was so different than Daren though, super awkward. The boy next to him didn't have a hint of awkwardness about him. He had strong arms and was tall. Not Jared tall, but he was tall. Now that I thought about it, Daren's brother was a swimmer.

"Wait a moment and I'll have your hot chocolate. I have to grab some cream from the back," the barista said.

I moved to the pick-up counter and opened Instagram on my phone. My feed was flooded with vacation photos from friends. Most of them were skiing or someplace warm like Florida or California. I checked Rainy's profile. Her most recent post was a family photo in front of the Christmas tree at her parent's house. I checked her stories, clicking through several photos of her morning breakfast and Starbucks order, a video of clouds floating past a round plane window, and another video of her doing a belly flop onto her bed back in our apartment.

"Madison." she greeted. The words were cool. I forced a smile on my face when I looked up from my phone at Winnie. She didn't even fake it. She looked annoyed that she was talking to me even though she had gotten up from her table of friends just to walk over to the counter.

"Winnie. It's good to see you again," I said a little stiffly.

She scoffed. "Is it?" Is it really?" She sat her coffee down and leaned against the counter.

"Winnie," I groaned. "Are we really going to keep up whatever drama we had between us in high school?"

She looked like I'd just said the most insulting thing to her.

"I'm just here celebrating Dax and you walk in."

"Yeah. I'm getting a drink and then I'm leaving. It's not a big deal."

She put a hand on her hip and did that stupid pouty thing with her lips like a little girl who was just denied ice cream or something. Did I act like this in high school when we would go back and forth about our dumb drama? I probably did. Gross. If I could go back and time and slap sixteen-year-old Madison, I would.

"I tell you right after I broke up with my boyfriend and then I catch you with him. I try enjoying the gala, my favorite party of the whole year, and you show up with him. Then, he tells me that he has a new girlfriend—"

"He told you? Wait, did you ask him out?" I felt electricity buzz through my veins when I saw the angry flush on her cheeks. I gave up on making her jealous not long after I agreed to help Jared. I almost forgot about Winnie entirely and here she was, absolutely pissed that I was with her ex. Maybe I really could have it all.

"Does he know that you and I have history?" Winnie asked after taking a moment to recover.

That knocked all the wind out of my sails. She knew it too. I should've just told Jared the minute we met that I knew Winnie. Heritage City wasn't a big town and Heritage City Academy was smaller than his high school, so I was sure he'd put together that we at least knew each other in high school. He never asked me. He never asked if I knew his ex-girlfriend, but that doesn't mean I couldn't have told him. It wasn't like Winnie and I had just had first period together or something. We had a long feud through most of school. How did you even bring that up in conversation?

"Oh, Winnie Maxwell? I hated her. I put itching powder in her cheer shoes, and she put red paint on the butt of my favorite jeans."

I came out of my thoughts when the barista cleared her throat. She stood with my drink in her right hand, looking awkwardly from Winnie to me. She sat the to-go cup on the counter next to Winnie's and I took it before she had a chance to try one of her usual tricks.

"It was good seeing you, Winnie," I said and started for the door.

"Real relationships are based on honesty," Winnie said as I passed her.

I almost whirled around to shoot and insult right back at her, but I knew that it wouldn't stop there. Winnie always had to have the final word. That's why I kept walking all the way out the door and across the street where I got back into the Jeep. I was proud of the way I handled that. I was done playing the high school mean girl. I wasn't going to stoop to name-calling and cheap insults.

But I was still petty enough to freeze her coffee on the pick-up counter.

THE HIGH FROM my victory over Winnie Maxwell wore off the moment I pulled away from the curb. I couldn't stop hearing her voice in my ears and even worse, I knew she was right.

Real relationships are based on honesty.

"Are you okay?" Marlee asked.

I looked across the kitchen counter. She sat at the living room window with that book propped in her lap. She wore her Sinclair standard-issue Christmas pajamas. They were green flannel bottoms with a button-up top and we all had a pair.

Every Christmas, we picked what next year's color would be. I was outvoted yet again. No pink for me.

"I'm fine," I answered and looked around the kitchen like I had been standing in here for a purpose and not just zoning out about Winnie making a good point. Ugh. I hated her.

"Come sit," Marlee said and put the bookmark in the book and set it aside.

"I'm pretty tired."

"Sit with me." The way she said it made me freeze halfway to the stairs. It was the stern tone she used when she was ready to step up to an argument. No. Marlee didn't argue. She just stated harsh truths. I wasn't sure who was worse, Winnie Maxwell or my own little sister.

I went to the living room and sat in the armchair opposite her. The only light came from the lamp that stood tall over the side table. *Christmas as We Know It* sat in the middle of the table next to a glass of water, the front cover curled upward a little from reading. Her bookmark was so close to the back cover that I wondered just how many pages she had left.

"What have you been hiding?" Marlee asked.

All right, then. Why not get straight to it?

"Nothing now. I introduced everyone to Jared."

"Maybe *hiding* is the wrong word," she said and straightened up in her seat. "What are you not telling… someone."

"Someone?"

She shrugged. "I haven't been able to figure out who you're not telling your little problem to. I know there's a problem though."

"Are you sure you want to be a lawyer and not a detective?"

She narrowed her eyes at me as if to tell me to give it up and cut to the chase already. I was a terrible liar. That was well established, so there was no way to keep the truth from her. So, I did the only thing I knew how to do in times like this. I talked around the issue.

"I ran into Winnie Maxwell at the coffee shop on the way home."

Marlee let out a deep breath and nodded. Marlee was my only sister who got made fun of by Winnie. Margot was too popular with her being a soccer star and all. She was also well-liked. Marlee was so different from us, different from most people really, that she was an easy target. She never said a word back to Winnie and I regretted that I never said anything either. Marlee just kind of rolled her eyes at Winnie and her stupid games and went back to her books.

"What did she do?" Marlee asked.

I was just about to recycle one of the many Winnie Maxwell stories I had, but I spilled my guts instead. I knew Marlee wouldn't judge me. At least, she would never call me stupid for anything I said or did. When she criticized me, it never felt like a personal attack. It always felt like she was just analyzing one of her books or true crime documentaries. She listened as I explained it all from the beginning. She looked almost disinterested by the end of it, and I felt a little embarrassed for dumping it all on her. I was the oldest and somehow, I was always the one with the drama.

"You should tell him," she said.

I groaned. "Just tell him? It's not that easy."

"Why can't it be? Relationships are pretty straightforward. All you do is communicate about how you feel and be open to hearing how the other person feels. It really is that easy. Its people being afraid of sharing or what they might hear that make it complicated."

"When was the last time you went on a date?" I asked.

"You don't have to date around to know that. If that were the case, then you could teach the Masterclass on the subject."

Ouch. Okay. My knee-jerk reaction was to make some cutting remark about how weird she was, but I realized that was kind of what she was talking about. You had to share your feelings. You also had to be open to hearing the feelings of others.

"So, I just tell him?"

Marlee nodded.

"I just walk up to him tomorrow morning and tell him that his ex-girlfriend and I were at war all of high school?"

"I would start with the usual greeting and maybe a *how are you* before you launch into your story, but sure," Marlee said and picked up the book from the side table.

Was this what it was like to be so smart? Was she always up on her valedictorian pedestal, looking down at us trying to navigate the world the hard way and shaking her head while we did it? It made me a little mad, but also… That sounded kinda miserable.

"So, what's the verdict?" I asked as she opened the book. She gave me an annoyed look that slowly melted into a small smile.

"It's cute," she said. "It's nothing super deep or provocative but—"

"You like it, don't you," I said, unable to hold in my squeal.

"A little," she answered, cheeks blushing, and I could see from the twitch at the corners of her mouth that she was trying her best to contain her smile. I laughed and after a moment, I was glad to see her smile. I didn't see her smile like that very often.

I stood up and paused. Marlee didn't open the book, chewing on her lower lip like she wanted to say more.

"Thanks," I told her. "You're a good therapist, which means that none of this leaves this room." I pointed a threatening finger at her.

She crossed her heart with her right index finger and before I could take more than a few steps, she cleared her throat and said, "It'll be fine as long as you just explain it to him."

I turned to face her. I believed her. Marlee was usually right. Like, ninety-nine percent of the time. That didn't make the idea any easier to think about though. My brain was filled with all the reactions I might get, not that I could imagine Jared acting like most of those visions.

"You really think so?" I asked.

Marlee opened the book this time and groaned. "I'm a pretty good judge of character."

"Which means you like him," I said with a giggle. Marlee never liked any of the people I hung around with, even less the guys I went on dates with. Even Rainy, my amazing roommate, she thought was a little stuck-up.

"If you leave me alone, I can finish this book and let you borrow it tomorrow."

I almost laughed. Like I was going to read that entire thing in the next couple of days before I had to go back to college. I could think of a million other things I wanted to do, a few of them involving Jared and making my face heat in such a way that I gladly left her to read in the dark living room.

Chapter 19

I didn't tell Jared.

I chickened out big time, even though I knew Marlee was probably right. We were just having such a good time that I mostly forgot. Yes, I decided not to talk to him about it when I remembered again, but we only had so many days together before the long-distance thing started. Since that day I saw Winnie, I was starting to feel a lot of anxiety about our relationship. I felt insecure, like leaving Crescent Peak would be the end.

Jared noticed.

"You know what's more fun when you're apart than when you're together?" Jared asked with an ornery grin as he walked me to the Jeep after our lunch at the diner.

"What?" I asked, stopping at the pink door. He leaned against the passenger door of his silver Truck.

"Texting and FaceTime." He winked and burst into boyish laughter a moment after. I used my powers to direct the snow falling around us so the closest flakes flew into his face. He continued to laugh as he brushed the flakes from the scruff along his jaw.

I wanted to correct him. Texting and FaceTime held more importance when you were long-distance, sure, but showing up on your boyfriend's doorstep after he sent a dirty text was much better than imagining yourself doing that.

"I'm wearing gym clothes. I'm packing a dress and a pair of heels, so make sure your outfit at least includes a tie," I said and rose on my toes to kiss him.

"I'll pick you up at two," he said.

It had snowed almost every day this week. It was a thick powder, the perfect kind of snow for making snowballs or building a snowman. I passed a family of snowmen as I went farther up the mountain toward the cabin.

"You're back early," Dad said. How he knew what we were up to when he spent his whole day working was beyond me. He did know though, which was more than Mom could say.

"We're going out in a few hours," I said and reached for the tea kettle on the stove. "I just came back to change."

I poured the hot water into a mug and filled it with a hot chocolate mix. It wasn't my usual recipe, but it would do while I got ready for whatever Jared had planned.

"I don't think I've ever seen you get that dressed up in just a few hours. You spent all day getting ready for the Winter Solstice gala," Dad said and sipped on his mug of tea.

I mixed the powdered cocoa into the hot water.

"We sort of split the date," I said and sat my spoon in the sink. "He gets the afternoon, and I picked our plans for the evening. Now that I think about it, going to a nice restaurant after doing whatever he picked that involves wearing gym clothes might not have been the best idea."

Dad chuckled. "You could always stop by the house to clean up."

"I guess that's true." The idea had occurred to me while Jared and I were at lunch. I tried to get his plans out of him, but he wouldn't budge. He told me to wear whatever I normally would to the gym and that was it. I figured I'd need to stop somewhere to clean up enough to go to a nice restaurant afterward and it made the most sense to stop at our house since we'd be in Heritage City.

"I trust you," he said. I saw the hint of anxiety in his eyes. He let out a deep breath and went to the corner of the kitchen. He reached into a plastic bag and pulled out a square box and held it up for a moment for me to see. A moment was all I needed to suddenly wish I'd walked right past the kitchen and gone straight upstairs to get ready.

"Just in case," Dad said and tucked the box of condoms into my purse.

Out of sight, out of mind. Mostly.

"Thanks," I said and took a long drink of the hot chocolate.

We stood in the kitchen drinking out drinks for a while longer until the silence was weird. I left Dad to go upstairs and change. I hadn't picked my outfits for our date, which was so unlike me. Part of me was more nervous about this date than our night at the gala. It was our first real date as a couple. It was also the last one we'd have before I went back to Kent University.

Weirdly, it was easier to pick my dress for our dinner than what activewear I wanted to wear. I picked a simple black dress and decided that I could pin my hair up so I could hide the fact that it was a little sweaty from whatever activity Jared had planned. I set the dress and heels on my bed and went back to planning the athletic outfit.

After piecing together a couple of looks, I decided that the tried and true was the way to go. I picked my favorite pair of pink leggings, the ones with a little rouching on the butt to make it look fuller. Jared made the joke the first time we were out in Crescent Peak together that he liked a round butt, so the rest of the outfit kinda came together around that idea. I decided to pair my black cropped sweatshirt with the leggings. I took a shower, which seemed like a weird thing to do before going to potentially work out, and then spent the rest of the time doing my makeup and curling the ends of my ponytail.

A knock came at my door as I finished the last few pieces of hair.

"Jared's downstairs," Margot said as she came in. She appeared behind me in the bathroom doorway. "You look cute."

"Thanks. Jared said to wear gym clothes, so I just dressed it up a little," I said and pulled the curling iron from the plug-in.

Margot snorted. "A little?"

I ignored her joke and led the way downstairs. I could hear Jared talking with Dad and when I reached the bottom of the stairs, I was able to get enough of their conversation to tell that they were talking about football.

"You're a Patriots fan then?" Dad asked.

"I haven't been watching as closely as usual, but yeah," Jared said.

One more reason to like him. Dad loved the Patriots.

"Who's driving?" I asked.

Mom handed my purse to me and kissed my cheek. Dad clapped Jared on the shoulder.

"If you don't mind, I was hoping I could," Jared said.

"Okay, sure," I said and told Mom and Dad that I would be home late.

"You remember the garage code?" Mom asked.

"Yes."

"Then just be quiet as you come in. Your dad has an early Zoom call thanks to the time difference and I'm hoping to sleep in. I just finished a huge project and I'd like to reset before I talk about the next quarter."

I told them I'd be quiet on my way back in and Jared promised to drive safely. Then, we were out the door and backing out of the driveway. Just like most of our drives, he tuned the radio to a station playing old rock songs and we sang along to the ones we knew, which was every fourth one for me and just about every one for him.

"So, are you going to tell me where we're going now?" I asked as we passed the sign for Heritage City.

Jared laughed. "Nope."

"Why not?" I asked. "You made me dress up for something sporty, so I know that it's not coffee or a movie."

"Take a guess," he said and turned onto the main road.

I thought for a moment as I watched the cars pass by. The snowplows had been through recently, tossing the white powder into piles along the side of the road and the median. The temperature on the billboard for a bank said it was twenty-seven degrees.

"Nothing outside or you would've had me wear more layers," I said.

Jared let out a taunting hum. Instead of continuing down the main road another block, he pulled into the turning lane. The road led into a large parking lot where several shops were. There was a grocery store, a couple of clothing stores, and a large outdoor sports store.

"Shopping?" I asked.

"Look again," Jared laughed as we pulled into a spot in front of the large building.

The backdrop to the store's sign featured people playing different sports, a couple hiking, and an obstacle course. I realized after looking at the front doors that we were there for the obstacle course.

"We're doing that?" I asked and pointed to the sign. "Like those bounce houses?"

"It's a ropes course, so it's about twelve feet into the air at a minimum. So, a little different than your grade school carnival," Jared said and got out of the truck.

I got out and hurried around the truck bed to meet him. He took my hand, and we carefully navigated the patches of ice on the road. The automatic doors slid apart for us and we were greeted with a giant room full of everything from Nike and Adidas apparel to basketball goals and gym equipment.

"Is this place a gym or a store?" I joked as he led the way to a service desk.

"Both," he said. "I thought you lived in Heritage City?"

"Not since they built this," I said. When I was in high school, this building used to be a Big Lots.

Jared told the man at the desk that we needed passes for the climbing area. I could see the area at the very back of the store now. It was behind a glass wall and looked mostly empty. It was hard to tell between the groups of people exploring the clothing sections.

"Sign this," Jared said, pulling my attention away from the store.

I signed the waiver, not bothering to read it in case it made me rethink my decision to navigate an obstacle course twelve feet in the air. Then, Jared led me to the back of the store. The course spanned the entire back half of the store. The course started out low and led to the rafters where there were nets to climb, vertical climbing walls, ropes made to look like vines between platforms, and other structures that made me stop to wonder how anyone managed to climb them.

"Hope you aren't scared of heights," Jared said as he opened the door. A woman at the harness station looked up from her cell phone when we came in.

"I was the flyer in the basket toss in our cheer routine that won first place at a couple of competitions, so no worries there," I said.

"Why is it called a basket toss?" Jared asked and stopped at the harness station. The woman looked over both of us and then went back to her wall of harnesses without asking for our measurements.

"Grab your left wrist," I said, doing the same. With my left hand, I grabbed onto his right wrist and that's when he caught on. Our hands formed a kind of box between us. "Our hands are like a basketweave. The flyer's feet go on our hands and that's how she's tossed into the air. It's a flatter surface than if I had a foot and you had a foot."

"Makes sense," Jared said tugging on my arm so I had no choice but to step to his chest. He kissed my forehead and then stepped away when the woman asked if she could fit us while the college-aged boy explained the rules.

I fit easily into the harness she gave me. I cinched it close to my waist the way she showed me and found all the carabiners that would attach to the hooks as the boy explained how to tether myself to each point along the course. Jared switched harnesses twice before they found one that would both fit his muscles and accommodate his height.

By the time he was all set, the boy had finished his spiel and already moved on to his station halfway down the course. We went to the lowest point of the course, a set of floating stairs made to look like rocks. The woman stopped us to make sure we clipped ourselves to the tethers correctly before giving us the okay to continue.

"Ladies first," Jared said with an onery grin.

"You're the one who's been here before. You know the course better than I do."

"Go on. She's waiting," Jared laughed and nodded at the woman who already looked exhausted by us. I gave in and clipped myself to the tether, waiting until she gave her approval to start up the stairs. There was no guardrail, just a set of rough rocks that wound up a boulder. I stopped at the top where the next tether was, connecting it to my harness before disconnecting the first.

Jared joined me at the top of the boulder as I looked nervously at the next obstacle. It was a bridge that stretched from one boulder to another about six feet away. It didn't sound intimidating, but when you considered that the bridge was only a few feet wide…

Every thought flew from my brain when Jared put a hand on my left hip. I felt the scruff of his jaw at my left ear.

"It's a nice view from down there," he said.

I reached back and slapped his arm, getting a laugh in return.

I felt like Bambi on that frozen pond as I crossed the bridge. I probably looked even more ridiculous, but Jared was supportive regardless of how unsexy the act was. I waited on the boulder for him to cross, a little frustrated by how easily he made it look in half the time it took me.

"You make this look… boring," I said when he met me again.

He smiled. "Believe me, it's not boring from where I am."

This time, I grabbed the front of his harness instead of telling him off. Who was I kidding? I loved every minute of this.

"I might like this whole hiking, mountain climbing thing," I told him and then turned around to face the net ahead.

"I haven't been mountain climbing since college started. Well, I guess I did go over the summer back to a few spots," Jared said as I started to climb. "I've climbed almost all the Fourteeners."

I scrambled to the platform at the top, clipping myself to the next section of the course so he could start on the net.

"That's cool. My family have lived in Heritage City my whole life and we've never done any of the outdoorsy things. Though I had some friends at school who would go glamping."

"Glamping," Jared scoffed as he climbed the net, not even breaking a sweat.

"Yeah. You know, when you go in an RV or something." I giggled a little as I realized who I was talking about. Most of my classmates went out of state for our school holidays, like to the beach or one of the big cities. Logan Norton's week in his family's RV watching the Denver Bronchos on their big screen over Thanksgiving wasn't near the same as what Jared was used to.

Jared pulled himself onto the platform. "Would you do Grays Peak with me? It's one of the easiest ones."

Instead of answering right away, I turned and started across the tight rope, using the rope above me for balance. Weirdly, this section was a little easier than the last two. Maybe I was just adjusting. It didn't take me as long to reach the next platform. I changed tethers and watched as Jared began to navigate the rope.

"Put it on our list of dates," I said, watching the smirk spread across his face.

Jared joined me on the platform, and we fell into a rhythm. I crossed the element first and then he would, much more gracefully than I had. The worst part was the rock wall. I couldn't figure out which handholds to grab until Jared directed each of my moves. It was the tallest point in the entire course. I could stand at full height and was only a few inches from scraping my head on the roof. Jared stayed on all fours when he joined me.

"I'm going to be sore tomorrow," I said and sat down next to him.

He took my hand and said, "It's not a view, but imagine you just climbed to the top of Gray's Peak and you're looking down at the trees below."

It was easy to picture. I thought about our hike in Crescent Peak. The river below flowed with icy water. I used my power to make a tree of ice that sat perfectly in Jared's palm.

I was brought back to the top of the ropes course when I felt Jared's lips at my neck. When I tipped my head away from him, giving him more access, he wrapped a hand around my waist and pulled me closer. I turned mine to find his lips and the kiss grew deeper. He leaned back on his forearm, and I had just started to lower myself toward him when the woman called to us on the speaker system.

"Ten minutes left."

Jared smiled against my lips, making me break the kiss and pull away.

"She probably saw us on the cameras," he said with a laugh.

"Jared!" I gasped and pushed away. He laughed, turning as red in the face as I felt.

"Let's go," he said and pulled me into a sitting position.

I went down the climbing wall and down the zipline in record time. When I finished the final two obstacles, I practically leaped out of the harness and tossed it into a bin before waiting on Jared to do the same. Then, before facing any awkward moments with the workers, we hurried out the door of the ropes course and went straight out the front of the store, hand in hand.

Chapter 20

Jared pulled onto the main road again, soft rock music playing on the radio.

"Turn on Baker's Street," I said. "We can go change at my parents' house."

"Are you in the gated area?"

I hesitated before confirming the fact. Baker's Heights was a gated addition where all the doctors, lawyers, and people like my parents lived. Basically, most of Heritage City Academy's families lived within those gates.

"I am guessing that we are going to a fancy dinner," Jared said as the trees opened, and we reached the outside gates of the addition. We continued a few blocks before we reached the main entrance.

"I'm not saying a word," I said. I unbuckled myself from the seat when he pulled up to the keypad. I leaned across him to type the number. I hit the zero instead of the eight when his hand rested on the back of my thigh. He dragged his thumb over the material of my leggings, back and forth until I quickly typed in the code, and the gate swung open.

"Now what?" he asked as he slowly passed the gate.

I looked his way, imagining where his hands would've gone if I'd messed up that code one more time...

"What? Dinner," I answered.

He gave me that onery smirk again and laughed.

"I meant which way to get to your house?"

My face burned. "The second right."

"We'll get you a cold glass of water when we get there," he laughed.

I groaned. "You can't do those things. It's distracting," I laughed.

"And what things do you mean, Madison?" Jared said with a challenging smile. I always knew he was the competitive type. I couldn't pass up a challenge and I wasn't going to give in that easily.

"Turn into the third gravel drive," I said.

I felt a little satisfaction when I saw his playful smile fade a bit. He turned into the driveway, and I heard a little gasp of surprise when he saw the boathouse, the pond, and the giant house at the end of the long driveway. He stopped in the driveway and put the truck in park. He took both our outfits from the back of the truck while I went to the garage to type the code into the panel.

The door rolled upward to reveal the mostly empty garage. He eyed Marlee and Margot's Jeeps, both of them parked on the far side of the garage as we walked to the door. I clicked the button on the wall and the garage slid shut again before we went inside to the kitchen.

I went to the far cabinet where the glasses were and filled two with cool water from the fridge. Jared took the class and leaned against the countertop, taking in the large space. I felt a pit forming in my stomach at the look of awe on his face.

Was coming here a bad idea?

"I know it's... extra," I said and dragged my foot over the kitchen floor. It looked newly polished. It probably was. My parents never suspended their cleaning service. Even when they were away for weeks at a time, they had a team come in almost weekly. It was my mom's love of order.

"I would love the grand tour," Jared said and motioned toward the living room.

I smiled nervously and led the way. The living room was complete with two sitting areas, one with two beige couches in front of the TV over the mantle that was flanked by built-in bookshelves that held family photos and décor pieces. The other sitting area had a gold bar cart that served as a side table between two tan chairs with chevron throw pillows. There was a couch under the window opposite the chairs that was known as Dad's napping couch.

I showed Jared farther down the hall where the den was, mostly a wall of books with an area dedicated to Dad's collection of scotch and Denver Broncos memorabilia. We peeked into Mom and Dad's offices, two separate rooms because they would never be able to share a space and get any work done.

Then, it was off to the upstairs area where the bedrooms were. I decided not to go too far down the hallway. I pointed out all our bedrooms and stopped at the first at the top of the stairs, which was the guest room that was only ever used when Grandma visited, or when my sisters and I had large sleepovers when we were younger.

"It has a bathroom and there's shampoo and stuff and towels if you want to shower before we go out again." I rambled as he walked around the space.

The bed was king-size and there was still enough space in the room for a dresser and sitting area that was composed of two armchairs and a small round coffee table. The attached bathroom was the smallest in the house, no tub in this one.

"This is great," Jared said and turned from the bathroom doorway to look at me. "Are you okay?'

He crossed the room and slid his arms around my hips. His

touch was reassuring. It made me feel more confident in admitting what was bothering me.

"I just feel a little…" I let out a sigh. "I know I have more than most people and I don't want you to think I'm taking it for granted. I know this house is amazing. It feels a little overwhelming after living in my three-bedroom college apartment with Rainy."

Jared smirked and tugged me closer.

"Is Rainy your roommate?" he asked.

"Yeah. She's a total badass. I want to be more like her."

Jared laughed and said, "You are pretty badass yourself, you know? You have high standards, and I don't mean that because your family has money. There's a difference between high standards and expensive taste."

I rose onto my toes to kiss him on the nose. My body relaxed and it felt like I was buzzing. Everything felt so good. From the honest words and boyish humor to the way his hands felt on my skin, it was all just so good that I felt like I would float away.

"I'm going to go get ready," I said.

Jared dropped his arms from around me and I lifted my garment bag from the stack he'd sat on the bed. My room was the first on the right and I realized when I walked in that I'd left my wall of fairy lights behind my headboard turned on. Instead of turning them off, I took a moment to look over my room. It was a pink dream and I loved it, but I was suddenly struck by a thought that made my heart race.

Was this too girly to have a boy in?

I immediately tried to shake the thought by getting dressed. I changed from my gym clothes into the dress I'd brought. It was a knee-length dress with a black long-sleeved top that clung to my arms and waist. A pleated skirt with a big bow on the front hung loose around my thighs, the color of champagne. I changed my mind about my shoes after putting on the dress and swapped the nude heels for a black pair in my closet.

I redid my makeup, so it matched better and then pulled my hair from the ponytail. Luckily, the curls were still intact, and the loose style added a bit of casualness to the outfit. Once I finished, I had to search to find Jared. He'd left the guest bedroom and the house was big enough that it took me a minute to find him sitting in the living room.

He wore a pair of light-gray slacks with a white button-up shirt, a gray tie, and the navy blazer. He'd fixed his hair so that it was styled a little more to one side than normal. It was the perfect balance of perfection and skill and effortlessness and bedhead. His gray shoes were propped up on the coffee table and he immediately lowered them to the floor when he saw me, mouth parting and a smile forming.

"You look great," he said, eyeing me.

I was so caught up in the way he looked at me that it took me a moment to form any words.

"Lose the tie," I said.

He shrugged and started to remove the gray tie. "Done."

"I'm driving. We're taking Margot's Jeep," I said. It wasn't anything against his car. Where we were going, we would only be allowed at this time of night with a visitor's pass or a parking permit. All my family's cars had a permit sticker at the bottom of the windshields.

"Okay," Jared said and stood up. "I'm assuming we are heading to a fancy dinner. Are we going to McNellis or Heritage?"

"Neither," I said as I led the way back to the kitchen. I took the key for the Jeep from the hook and then went to the garage. Margot's blue Jeep smelled almost new when we climbed into it. It was pretty close to new. She'd gotten it during her senior year and then left it behind for California. There was no reason for anyone else to drive it until now.

"So, this is Margot's car," Jared said after I'd finished backing out and we were on our way toward the road.

"How did you know?" I asked. I looked his way and saw him holding a certificate. It had Margot's name at the top in big letters with the award of MVP underneath. It was from her soccer banquet senior year. "Where was that?"

"Under the seat." Jared shrugged and put the award back where he'd found it.

"We are going somewhere better than McNellis," I said.

"I already mentioned the two nicest restaurants in town. Where are we going?" Jared asked.

"You'll have to wait and see," I said in a sing-song voice.

Jared didn't press me. He played along, even though I was sure he had already figured out the secret. I pulled up to the gate for the country club, glad I was in the driver's seat this time, so I didn't have to worry about focusing with Jared's hands on my skin.

"Is there an event going on tonight?" Jared asked.

"They serve dinner most nights," I told him as the gate swung open. I drove through and took the next right toward the main building. The country club was lit with spotlights and twinkling Christmas lights on every bush along the road. I parked the car close to the doors. It looked like there was just a small crowd for dinner tonight, which was why I chose the country club over the other places in town.

I liked the idea of quiet.

"I've never been to the club," Jared said as he got out of the car.

"It's usually pretty calm, which means the service is amazing. The food is just as good as anywhere in town," I said and then gasped. I grabbed onto his arm and added, "You'll want to order the scallops."

Jared laughed and held the front door open for me. "We'll order the scallops."

I led him down a hall to the left where the restaurant was. It wasn't a large dining area, just enough for a couple of dozen round tables, but they were all dressed to the nines. The far wall was mostly comprised of windows that overlooked the garden below, which was decorated with Christmas lights. We got a table right away, one next to the window.

"Such a nice view," Jared said and looked over the garden. "I bet you get deer during the early hours."

"We had a couple of them a few days ago," our waitress said as she filled the glasses on the table with water from a pitcher. "I'll give you a moment to look at the menu."

We ordered an appetizer, bruschetta, and I told Jared how Christmas at the Sinclair cabin went. I told him how proud of myself I was for getting Marlee a gift that she actually enjoyed. He told me about the new clothes his mom had bought him, and the cologne Mark gave him.

"I love that cologne, by the way," I said. My cheeks heated when he looked up from what was left of the bruschetta. "I like the way it smells on you."

He smiled and said, "I like the way your hair smells."

My hair? It took me a moment to remember what I used. I'd been buying the same shampoo for years. It came in a yellow bottle and was thick. It smelled like honey.

"Thank you," I said and stacked my plate on top of his and sat it on the edge of the table. A long silence fell over the table and we just stared at each other. I felt more aware of the low V of my dress. I cleared my throat and took a drink from my glass, hearing Jared's hum of a laugh.

"I don't know why I'm so nervous," I told him. "We've spent basically every day together and we've been out before..."

"I get it. I'm nervous too," Jared said.

It made me stop. He never once seemed nervous at all since he picked me up at the cabin. He actually seemed a little more confident than usual. I reached across the table, and he moved his hands so I could lace my fingers between his.

"Why are you nervous?" I asked.

He paused a moment before taking a deep breath. He gave my hands a gentle squeeze, keeping his eyes on them for a second. He checked to make sure no one was around. There was just one other couple in the entire restaurant and the staff seemed to be occupied by something near the kitchen, all of them gathered there to look over an iPad. Jared looked back at me and lowered his voice.

"Everything has been so good, and it just feels like the most natural next step… I don't want you to think that I'm moving things along too fast. I was worried that you wouldn't be ready and that it would ruin things if I even made the move…" His cheeks were growing pinker by the second. My heart had picked up speed. It skipped when he looked anxiously up at me.

"I'm sorry. There was a mix-up in the kitchen," our waitress said as she returned with an iPad in her hands. "I can take your order if you are ready, but it will be a bit before the entrees come out. I want to offer you another appetizer or a dessert on the house." After pushing all the right buttons, she looked up at us.

Jared and I had sprung apart when she returned. My hands were already working on the zipper of my purse. I pulled out my wallet and a fifty-dollar bill.

"We had something come up also," I told her and held out the bill. "I don't need any change. Thank you."

I stood up and after recovering from the shock, so did Jared. My heart thundered in my chest as I led the way out of the restaurant and toward the entrance of the building. Jared caught my hand once I reached the front steps and he burst into laughter. I couldn't help but join in, towing him toward the parking lot where we were quick to climb into the Jeep and buckle ourselves in.

"I'm glad I didn't scare you away," he joked as I put the car in reverse.

"I've been waiting for you to make that move all night," I said.

I drove a little quicker than I probably should've considering the weather. We were back at the house with Margot's Jeep parked in the garage in minutes. Jared was already slipping out of his blazer as we moved through the kitchen. I didn't stop to look back at him until I reached the top of the stairs.

He froze halfway up. He'd kicked his shoes off along the way, his blazer somewhere downstairs so he was dressed only in his slacks with his shirt untucked. I turned and went into the guest bedroom, tossing his gym clothes onto the floor.

Jared's gym clothes fell in a heap at the end of the bed, leaving the mattress clear. I turned to find him standing in the doorway. I knew he was tall, but there was nothing like filling a doorway to remind a girl of the fact. His head was just a few inches shy from brushing the top and his broad shoulders put him inches away from the sides as well. I felt suddenly nervous. It wasn't like it was the first time I'd ever had sex, but I'd never had sex with anyone like Jared and it had been just long enough that the idea made butterflies fill my stomach.

I took a deep breath and gathered the hem of my dress. Before I could lift it past my hips, Jared joined me and brushed my hands away. He looked down at me again before pressing a kiss to my forehead.

"If it's alright with you," he said and stepped back. "I'd like to do that part."

My heart skipped in my chest. I nodded and rested my hands against his chest, running my fingers over the buttons of his dress shirt.

"Can I…"

Jared nodded and said, "Ladies first."

I started with the top button, the butterflies in my stomach taking flight when I undid the first two buttons to expose the hollow of his throat. I paused to rise up on my tiptoes and press a kiss to that soft spot. I continued to unbutton his shirt, fumbled a little as my nerves caught up with me with every extra inch of exposed skin under my fingers. I tugged the hem free from his pants and let the shirt hang open. I slid my hands up his bare chest and over his shoulders, guiding the sleeves down his arms until the shirt fell to the floor behind him.

"Nervous?" he asked and captured my hands as I rested them against his chest.

"I've wanted to do this for a while," I said. "That's all."

Jared smiled and said, "Are you sure?"

"Remember what I said about not wanting a gentleman?" I reminded him, slapping my hand playfully against his chest.

He smirked and lowered his hands. They went to my hips, sliding around to the back of my waist and then over the curve of my butt. He gave the right side a tight squeeze before pulling me to him. He pressed his hips against me so I could feel how sure he was about taking the next step.

"Your turn, Elsa," he said.

I unbuckled his belt and pulled it free from the loops of his slacks. I draped it around his neck and used it to pull myself onto my toes to reach his lips. He melted against me, mouth parting and the kiss growing deeper until I thought my heart would beat out of my chest. He smiled against my lips before pulling back a fraction.

"The ice queen has tricks," he said, moving his hands from my waist to my hands on the belt. He took the two ends from me and lifted it over his head, over mine, and let it scoop under my butt so I was lifted onto my toes. He hoisted me up until I was at eye-level and my legs were wrapped around his hips. He tossed the belt onto the bed and his hands slid up my thighs, under the hem of my dress, looping his fingers under the fabric as he went so it rose up my hips and over my torso until he pulled it over my head and tossed it aside.

"I like your trick better," I said as his lips went to my neck, leaving a trail of soft kisses from my jaw down my neck and over my collarbone.

"That wouldn't have worked if you didn't have a little bit behind you," he said and slapped my butt. "I wouldn't have taken you for a thong kind of girl."

"What does that mean?" I asked with a giggle. He smirked and lowered me onto the bed. I pulled him closer with my legs, forcing him to climb on top of me.

"It means that I'd really like to get out of these pants," he said and cupped the side of my face.

"Okay," I said and pulled him closer by the nape of his neck.

He laughed and indulged me with a sweet kiss before he pulled back just enough to stand up. He let his slacks pool at his ankles and stepped out of them, nudging them to the side. Everything inside of me sped up as I watched him slide his briefs down. My entire body heated up and I felt light, like I might float away, until he reached for my hips and towed me to the edge of the bed.

I let out a squeal of surprise, the sound abruptly cut off when Jared leaned over me again. I drew in a shaky breath as he cupped the side of my face with one hand, eyes alight with desire. His other hand rested gently against the side of my neck. Just like he had at the gate hours before, he began to lightly drag his fingertips over my skin. Slowly, so slowly, too slowly... They ran down my chest, between the space between my breasts, down my stomach where they stopped at the elastic band of my thong. I lifted my hips toward him, but he kept his touch light as he traced along the waistband from one hip bone to the other.

"Are you sure you want this?" he asked softly. "I want to hear you say the words."

Ugh! The way my body melted at the words.

"Yes," I said.

"Are you really, really sure?" he asked with a teasing smile, dipping his fingers just past the elastic and continuing to trace from hip to hip.

"Ugh! Jared, yes," I said with a giggle that was immediately cut off in a gasp when he slid his hand further, fulfilling every secret dream I'd had of that delicate touch.

He smiled, an ornery look that had me a little concerned he might pull away before I was ready. He didn't. He continued with soft strokes until it was nearly too much and then moved his hand from my face to the waistband of my thong and slid it down my thighs in a single motion. He leaned over me, his face inches from mine and the rest of him filling the space between my legs. I bit down on my lower lip as I adjusted to the feeling.

"Alright?" he asked, pulling my lip from my teeth with his gentle thumb.

"Perfect, " I said and angled my hips to meet his. With that one word, he began to move and there was nothing left to say. Everything really was perfect.

Chapter 21

THERE WASN'T a TV in the guest room, so after a while, we redressed and went to the media room at the end of the hall to watch a movie and snuggle under a fluffy blanket. At some point, we fell asleep there, because I woke up at four in the morning with the TV frozen on the message from Netflix asking if we were still watching.

Jared was a heavy sleeper. He didn't budge when I rose from the couch and went to my bedroom. I went straight to the bathroom and was shocked at how horrible I looked. My mascara was smeared over my cheeks. One eye looked like I'd completely removed the eyeshadow I had on while the other still had all the bronze and gold shadow in place. How long had I looked like this? Had I gotten out of the guest bed with my makeup half off?

Probably.

I tried to forget about it and decided to shower. I left the door to the bedroom open as I started the water so the room wouldn't get too steamed up. When I finished, I dressed in a pair of jeans and a sweater I sat out on the counter. I didn't have any makeup with me, so I settled for blow-drying my hair and pulling it into a ponytail.

I was surprised when I went back into my bedroom to see

Jared standing at my wall of photos. Then, I remembered what I hadn't told him. The panic set in.

"I figured you knew her, but..." Jared turned from the wall and then pointed at it with a finger. "You and Winnie were on the cheerleading team together."

"Yeah," I answered. "We were."

"All of high school?" Jared asked.

"Yeah."

He turned to the wall again, studying the photos more in-depth and touching the ones that featured big groups. There was a team photo for all four years, Winnie and I standing on opposite sides. There was a photo of our team stunting, Winnie held high in the air on the right and me held up on the left. I had a few pictures in the mix with my high school friends.

"Did you not recognize her when she caught us at the farm? She looks mostly the same to me," Jared said.

His sincerity was heartbreaking considering what high school had been like between Winnie and me. I was distracted enough by his question that I hadn't noticed him pick up one of my yearbooks from the desk until he had it open and was flipping through the pages. I rounded the bed to try sliding it from his hands.

"I looked horrible in high school..." I started and held out my hand.

Jared turned his back on me, and I could see past his elbow that it was open to a two-page spread dedicated to the HCA cheer team. It was my senior year. There were four photos on the pages. One was the entire team lined up together. Another was an action shot that featured us on the sidelines with our poms held high and everyone doing a high kick. The entire second page was reserved for the seniors on the team.

That year, Winnie and I were the only seniors. We posed side-by-side. I had one arm around Winnie's shoulders and the other perched on my hip. Petty, seventeen-year-old Madison had drawn devil horns on Winnie and a mustache. Above her, I'd written a single sentence.

Winnie Maxwell is a two-faced bitch and a boyfriend stealer.

IT WAS ALL TRUE. Well, mostly. I forgot about what happened with my senior-year boyfriend. I dated Noah that fall, and we broke up. Winnie was hanging off his arm a month later. At the time, it felt better to say she stole him from me. She'd done what she always had and got her way when she didn't deserve it, especially when I was involved. The truth was that Noah said I was too much drama and that he needed to focus on raising his SAT to get into college.

I felt the moisture in my eyes. Jared was staring at that page. I was sure he was reading the message over and over. I waited for him to say something because I didn't know what I would say. It seemed like nothing would fix this. I could promise I was different now. I could tell him all the ways I was different now, but would he believe them after how our relationship started?

"Jared," I said, my voice a whisper.

"You more than knew her," he said and shut the yearbook. He sat it on the desk and turned to look at me. I could see his eyes glisten for a moment before he sucked in a deep breath and looked at me.

"I didn't make the connection that she was your ex until you helped me with the axe," I said.

"You went along with the plan and didn't tell me you hated her," he said, the hurt in his voice growing with each word.

"You're the one who wanted to lie about being in a relationship to make her jealous."

"Is that what you were doing? Did you want to piss her off

by dating her ex, the same way you say she did?" Jared pointed to the yearbook.

"It crossed my mind, but—"

Jared groaned. "Crossed your mind," he said under his breath.

"You did the same thing!" I said.

He shook his head and said. "I was upfront with you from the beginning. I told you I wanted to make her jealous to win her back. I was the one who admitted I had feelings for you. I was the one who made that first move."

"Everything I feel is real. Jared, I loved every minute we were together from the first day. I didn't do all of this because of her."

"But you didn't tell me," Jared said.

I didn't say anything. He was right about that. It didn't change anything. It didn't change that I loved him or that I felt like I could take on the world when we were together. I'd been dreading the moment I went back to Kent ever since.

"If you had just given up on our stupid agreement to have a real relationship, then why didn't you just tell me?" His tone was soft.

"I-I don't know. I wanted… I'm not that girl anymore and I just wanted to put that as far behind me as I could," I said, trying to keep the tears from falling.

He scoffed.

"Our actions and our intentions are two different things," he said. "You and Winnie seem pretty similar to me."

Jared looked back at me for a long moment, the hurt plastered on his face. He slowly made his way back to the guest bedroom and I followed him at a distance. He pulled the navy blazer on and stuffed the tie in the pocket. He tucked his wallet in the pocket of his slacks and then lifted the keys from the bed, twisting the keyring in his fingers for a long moment.

"Don't tell me that this is how we end things." I said. "I don't want them to end."

Jared stopped fidgeting with the keys and clasped his right hand around them.

"I don't know," he said. "I need to think."

He looked back at me. I brushed a tear from my cheek, and he looked away again.

"I can take Margot's Jeep back to Crescent Peak," I told him.

He stood there another minute before he nodded. He passed me in the doorway and went down the stairs. I waited with a knot in my chest until I heard the door close from the kitchen to the garage. A couple minutes later I could see the silver truck driving away through the window above the stairs.

THE SILENCE around the cabin was painful. How did Marlee spend all of winter break this way? How all her books were enough of an escape from the white noise of the wind outside and the hushed arguments between Mom and Dad was beyond me.

It must have been obvious, thankfully, what had happened because no one asked me a single question when I arrived back at the cabin in Margot's blue Jeep and went straight upstairs. I spent most of the next day in my room, trying to distract myself with shirt designs and website work. When I was tired of the same four walls and moved into the living room the next day, Margot was the only one who looked at me with any amount of pity.

I looked up from the living room window as Marlee stopped in front of my armchair. She sat a book in my lap. It was *Christmas as We Know It.*

"It's a good escape from everything," she said.

"Good?" I asked, challenging her to explain.

She rolled her eyes. "Good for a romance."

"You mean good for something that's not by Jen Austen?"

"It's *Jane* Austen," Marlee groaned. "How do you not know that? Didn't you do a book report on *Pride and Prejudice*?"

I did, but I remember making a C and I had watched the movie with Kiera Knightly.

"Thanks," I said and held up the book with both my hands. Marlee offered a small smile and went back to the stairs to disappear again for the rest of the day like normal.

I had to get out of there.

I took the book with me. I wasn't sure where to go. I didn't want to run into anyone I knew, and I wanted to go somewhere private. I drove around Crescent Peak a few times, checking out all the usual spots. The diner would be packed. The coffee shop would be too. It didn't make sense to sit in the other shops downtown. I took the road up the mountain where the snow thinned out and the pavement went from dusted in white to bone dry.

The lodge was practically abandoned. The parking lot was empty, and I could see farther down the road that many of the cabins on the property were empty too. A lot of the guests had only come for the winter solstice. I parked in one of the front rows and went to the front doors.

I was a little nervous that they'd closed the main building for the season, but the door pulled open with a strong tug. The giant room within had been cleaned from the party and the floors were polished. The outdoor chairs that had sat on the deck were moved inside and stacked in a corner. I pulled one from the stack and moved it near the back door so I could see the tip of the highest peak, and I started chapter one of the book.

Marlee was right. It was a good escape. I was worried about reading any kind of romance after everything that had happened but diving into someone else's romantic drama eased the pain of my own and it became the norm over the next few days.

I stopped avoiding my family and actually went out to lunch at the diner with Marlee and Margot. It was quieter than usual inside. The entire town was quiet. I had spent so much time in my own little bubble that I didn't realize the date until I looked down at my phone just then. We were all flying out in a week and the spring semester at Kent would start a few days after.

Dread filled my gut as I thought about the classes I was enrolled in. When did I get so bored? The subjects just felt too simple— I knew they weren't. I wasn't that jaded. Still, the idea of any of the classes I had left to take that started with the word *fashion* or *design* felt shallow. I was taking a fashion marketing class this semester. *That* seemed interesting and was the only thing aside from Rainy that I looked forward to.

"We should do something fun before we fly out," Margot said as the waiter placed her BLT before her. I thanked the man for my salad and Marlee immediately dipped a piece of her bread into her tomato soup.

"We should. I'm down," I said. The more distractions I could set up, the better. I only had a few chapters left of my book.

"Like…" Marlee said as she dipped another hunk of bread in the soup.

"We could probably rent skis at the lodge Dad likes," Margot said.

Marlee's face said it all.

"What about a hike? I know a place," I said, knowing it wouldn't change Marlee's attitude at all. This was more of a Margot and Madison kind of adventure.

"How about I catch up with you guys for hot chocolate after?" Marlee asked.

Margot shrugged. "I like that. Tomorrow?"

"Yeah. Tomorrow," I said and stabbed my fork into the bowl of spinach.

Chapter 22

Thankfully, Margot let me sleep in. She had been up since four and had done an entire workout before I met her in the living room in my pink pants and thick sweatshirt. We finished our looks with puffy coats and hats before loading up in my Jeep to make the trip up the mountain.

I remembered the entire way, making as much conversation as I could as we drove to try to rid myself of the memories of Jared's terrible singing.

"Where did you get those boots?" Margot asked when she came around the front of the Jeep to join me at the trailhead.

I looked down at them, nearly brand-new looking other than the single spec of mud dried on the toe from their last hike on this trail.

"The outdoor store in Crescent Peak," I answered with a shrug.

"Since when do you *own* hiking boots?" Margot joked.

I led the way toward the trees where the sign for the trail was. We'd gotten so much snow recently that the entire trail was covered in a thick layer of it that crunched satisfyingly under my boots.

"You guys always talk like I'm some stupid blonde," I moaned. "It's like I didn't do cheer. It wasn't just the same chants with a few jumps thrown in like it was at HCA, I went to national competitions with the private team. I had abs of steel."

Margot stopped laughing and her smile slipped into a frown.

"I'm sorry. I didn't mean anything. It was just a joke."

"I know that," I said and kicked at the snow. It didn't rise into the air like the soft powder I expected. It flew into the wooden post of the sign in a compact ball. We kept going in silence for a few minutes. The hike was going to be harder than when I'd done it with Jared thanks to the thick snow.

"Margot, am I still that bitch from high school?" I finally asked.

The crunching of feet stopped, and I looked back at her shocked expression.

"Is that what happened?" she asked, cheeks turning red. "Did he call you that?"

"No. No, that's not it," I said quickly and then turned to hike on. "Well, not really. He didn't say that. He just implied that I was the same as…"

I stopped walking again and took a deep breath. Margot joined me, waiting intently for me to continue.

That's when I told her the truth.

I started from the beginning, from the moment I decided to stop at the mercantile on the way to the cabin. When Winnie came into the story, I told her everything that had happened between us at the skating rink. I told her about the wreaths, meeting the McAdams, our dates, and when we both admitted that our relationship was real. She never said a word, not even when I told her about our argument in my bedroom.

"Wow," Margot said under her breath as we walked.

I nodded. The movement up the slope made my heart beat fast for a different reason than the story and I welcomed it. It made me feel in control in a way I wasn't when it came to Jared and me.

"You're not the same bitch from high school, to answer your question," Margot said.

"How would you know, other than the obvious," I said. Her confused expression prompted me to elaborate. "You're my sister. You know my history. You knew me better than anyone. How would *he* know that I'm not the same person?"

"Oh. Easy," she said with a harumph. "You're nice. You do things for others. You let Mom and Dad spoil you, but you never ask for anything. You paid the rent on your apartment the first two months before Mom and Dad realized you'd moved out of the dorms. You aren't the gossip queen anymore. You used to have nothing to talk about except other people."

"But Winnie—" I started.

"Winnie Maxwell is infuriating enough to make anyone a little petty."

"He's right though. I wanted something out of our relationship too. I was using him to piss her off and didn't tell him. Doesn't that say something?"

Margot walked in silence for a moment.

"I think…" Margot spoke slowly, as though still deciding how to answer. "We aren't defined by our pasts. We are defined by our choices moving forward."

"And I chose to use Jared without him knowing."

Margot shook her head. "You made a bad choice because you were caught in an awkward situation with Winnie catching you and Jared. You went along with the story, yes, but you chose him over Winnie."

We'd reached the top of the trail where the metal bench was, only it was so covered in snow that you could barely tell what it was. I went to the railing and then turned around to look at Margot. Not even the beautiful scenery could ease my stress about the situation.

"I did go along with it."

"Madison, if you had gone along with the idea to piss off

Winnie then you would've paraded Jared around Crescent City the whole time instead of going on those outdoorsy dates and trips out of town."

"I brought him to the gala to show him off," I said.

"Yeah, and we were all really impressed by him," Margot said with a laugh. "But what was Winnie Maxwell wearing that night?"

I had no idea. I wasn't concerned with her that night. I'd been so focused on the dance and not turning to mush at the idea of being that close to Jared.

"High school Madison would never have even stuck out the fake relationship. Guys like Jared just do their own thing, stick to themselves, and stay close to home… You kept going not because you made that bogus agreement so he wouldn't tell everyone you were a witch, but because he was interesting to you. High school Madison would've been bored the first day."

There was that word. Bored. It was just like Winnie said. She broke up with him because she thought he was boring. She wanted everything my parents had. They traveled all over the place. Mom dropped thousands in a single store on things she already had but in a different color. Dad went on expensive outings to country clubs and golf courses to impress whatever business guy he was working with now. It all screamed of luxury and *that* was boring to me. It was exhausting trying to keep up and it was unattainable for anyone who didn't already have it.

Stupid.

"Madison, did you really think he was going to tell everyone you're a witch?" Margot scoffed.

I shrugged. I never thought much about how it would play out. I worried he would, but I never was realistic.

"I can't," she said and burst into fits of laugher. "I'm imagining Jared walking into the diner and accusing you of witchcraft. Just imagine him for a moment. First, Jared would never call out anyone like that. It's just not his thing to get justice when he can just leave the situation. Second, what would they say? Start the pyre, let's burn her now?"

I laughed at the last part, and we started the decline, wracking our brains for any real instance of a witch being outted in this century. We couldn't think of a single example.

AFTER HOT CHOCOLATE at the café, Marlee, Margot, and I ended up walking in and out of the stores in Crescent City until we went back to the cabin for dinner. It was a non-event filled with sandwiches and Mom on the phone with someone at work who apparently couldn't fix a problem that she should be able to in her position. It had Mom heated and Dad started to mumble about how the person should never have been hired to begin with if they couldn't do the basics.

That was how our planned dinner of Mom's famous cinnamon chicken turned into sandwiches and dinner in our bedrooms.

I looked through all my university accounts as I ate, checking for any posts from my teachers next semester and even checking the availability of other classes. Surprisingly, and frustratingly, I didn't have any business classes left to take. That led me to looking deeper into what classes I had left for my degree and their descriptions on the Kent State class cataloged page.

I had the page for the University of Colorado open to their business program before I realized why I had chosen that school. I'd taken one of the classes listed and all the required general education requirements aside from a humanities class. I wouldn't really be that far off track if I switched majors. I could take some classes over the summer and take an extra this semester. That should put me back on track to graduate on time.

I shut my laptop after I'd looked over the transfer process as Jared came through my mind. Was I thinking about moving home because of Jared? I knew it wasn't to be near my dysfunctional parents. Or was I moving back for more?

I looked over the University of Colorado website more than once the next two days. I found my fingers going there unintentionally when my mind wandered from all the website work. I'd decided by the end of the week that I would drop a couple of my fashion classes and add a few business ones to test the waters. I knew I would like them. I was so sure that I was nearly ready to switch my major entirely.

"I'm going out," I said with *Christmas as We Know It* in my hand and my coat half on. Marlee was the only person sitting in the living room to hear me and she didn't bother to look up from her laptop, so I forged ahead.

It was colder than I expected. The temperature had dropped dramatically overnight and the frost over the driveway was frozen into swirls and zigzags in a way that made the concrete look like granite as I backed out. Where I was headed, the roads were spotless and the lodge was warm.

I drove slowly until I reached those dry roads that curved up the mountain. The lodge was once again empty. No one had bothered to de-ice the parking lot, so I just pulled up to the front curb and parked. I got out with my book in hand and quickly went into the building to get away from the frigid air.

I knew I was going to finish the book that day. I only had three chapters left to read. I thought about not even leaving the house and just finishing it in my bedroom, but the idea of sitting still in that cabin for another hour made me restless. I moved my usual chair from the window to the far side of the room where the food was usually set up. There was a large fireplace in the corner and after looking over the stone and the logs sitting inside, I figured out how to turn on the gas.

The flames whooshed to life so quickly that it made my heart beat fast. I adjusted the flames to keep the area from getting too warm and then I settled into my chair and propped my feet on the fireplace. The last chapters were quick, probably because I was dying to read them. I needed to know how things ended. I sat and thought about the main characters for a long time. Jason had been such a grouch the entire book. Well, not the entire book, but I didn't like him in the beginning. I understood him now.

Maybe I wasn't the only person who had grown.

I pulled my phone from my pocket and sat my feet on the floor as I typed out my message.

I SAT BACK and waited for the reply. I let my mind wander to the characters again. It was another ten minutes before Winnie sent a text back.

Chapter 23

WHEN I PULLED up to the curb at the café, I parked behind Winnie's black SUV. I could see her sitting inside the giant window with a cup of coffee on the table. I gathered my purse and got out of the Jeep.

The store was almost overly warm when I stepped inside. The barista greeted me with a warm smile and asked what I wanted. I orded my usual hot chocolate with whipped cream and sprinkles, trying to forget about the last time I had a cup with Winnie.

"This better be an apology," Winnie said when I slipped into the seat opposite her.

I sucked in a deep breath to make sure my tone didn't undermine my entire reason for being here.

"It is, but not for the reason you think," I said and watched her frozen expression. She glared back at me for a long second before letting out a sigh and sitting back in her seat. She looked out the window.

"This is about everything before," she said under her breath.

"Yes, and I don't know how you feel about it all, but I feel terrible. We were so mean to each other, and I don't know why other than that we were constantly in competition. I just wanted to let you know that I had tried moving past all of that and having relationships with people that weren't about me being in control or being the one with the most money." I hated that my eyes burned as I thought about it all. I could hear Jared's tone in my head, that one that implied that I was a bitch.

Winnie kept her eyes on the snow that started to fall outside the window. She snorted.

"You always did come out on top," she said under her breath.

"Me? Anytime I won anything at school or had anything that was mine, you came in and took it away or beat me on a technicality," I shot back. This was a bad idea.

"A technicality," she muttered before looking straight at me. She wasn't mad the way her tone suggested. Or, if she was, her expression didn't match that. She looked like I was dragging up the worst memory.

"I had the better cheer captain tryout. You have to know that," I said, forcing myself to lower my voice. "Our routines were almost identical except I threw a full in the tumbling pass and you threw a tuck. Coach Nora made us co-captains."

"Only because my dad had sex with her," Winnie said, the anger finally crossing her face.

"Oh," I said, struggling to keep our conversation on track. "Well, you won homecoming queen and threw that in my face. I was sick with the flu and wasn't at school the entire week that voting happened. You and the rest of the court got to go on stage and read off your advice to the underclassmen. No one even knew I was on the court."

Winnie shook her head as though I was missing the obvious piece.

"Coach Nora was senior sponsor," she said with a laugh. "That's how I won homecoming queen and prom queen. They had a whole relationship going that I just pretended I didn't know about while my mom was gone every weekend to take care of my grandma."

"I'm sorry," I said. I wanted to shoot back every insult she'd ever sent my way in high school, but that wouldn't help anything. She wasn't trying to take away the mean things she did. She was just trying to explain why she did them. "My parents aren't ever around. I sort of understand having the shitty dad thing. Mine care, but their version of showing it involves Gucci and Prada. It's dumb. They have more than most of the country and they work away at all hours like our rent depends on it. I know for a fact that it doesn't. I've seen their savings. They're fine."

Winnie nodded slowly. "I'm sorry too."

Her tone was so unlike what I was used to that it surprised me. I had to study her somber expression to make sure it wasn't sarcasm.

"I was always jealous of your sisters and friends," Winnie said. "Even when I got all those things it wasn't some victory. I found out about my dad after the co-captain thing, so that sucked. It ruined everything because I just let it all happen until my grandma passed and my mom found out herself. And prom queen... My own friends didn't congratulate me. Tasha didn't speak to me after that, and you know she was like the only person I ever spent time with. More like the only person who put up with all the drama."

I laughed. "I was always jealous that you got everything you wanted after I tried so hard. I worked so hard at cheer because it was something my mom thought was cool. She drove me to all the competitions and practices and would actually watch our routines instead of scrolling through her spreadsheets. The only people who ever thought about what I felt instead of what I won were my sisters. My friends weren't a ton better than Tasha. They acted like it, but I could tell they were just as jealous of my wins as I was of yours."

"It's so stupid now that I think about it," Winnie said and took a sip of her coffee.

"I know. I tried putting that all behind me and I am so

different now. At least, I try really hard to be different. When I ran into you at the skating rink…" I didn't need to explain any more. This was where things were different. From what Jared said and all the things Winnie had done since, how different was she really?

"I know you're different. I stalked your socials. I found your website," Winnie said as she looked down at her mug. She let out a groan and sat back. "That's what made me so mad. I was hoping you were… My parents split. My mom lives in an apartment. You know, the ones on Willow Street? I see my dad sometimes. He and Nora moved to Denver, and they try to do the whole two-families-are-better-than-one thing. It's better than it was, I guess."

We sat for a long time in silence. A couple came in and ordered coffee. They sat down across the café from us and started to look through something on the woman's phone. When I looked back at Winnie, she'd finished her coffee and was spinning the empty mug between her hands.

"Do you like Jared?" she asked.

I nodded. "A lot."

She gave a small smile. "It never would've worked with us. That's why I broke it off."

"You told me he was boring," I said.

"I know. He's not boring. We just like different things. I talked about where I see myself. I plan on staying in Denver or moving to another big city to join the business world. It wasn't until after I'd gotten so involved with organizations on campus and made a few connections with businesses in Denver that I realized I didn't see him with me anymore." She said and pushed the mug to the middle of the table. "You know what he likes. I think I just realized the differences between us before he did."

I thought about what she said for a second. Before I could reply, her eyes moved from my face.

"Speak of the devil," she said with a smile.

I followed her gaze to the door just as it opened and the little bell overhead tinkled. Jared stopped there with the snow blowing in over his shoulder. His expression fell when he saw me. He looked nervous, more nervous than I imagined he would when we met again. Something was wrong.

"You need to come with me, Madison," he said.

I didn't put my coat on as I stood up.

"I'm glad we talked," Winnie said, her expression sincere as I fumbled with the strap of my purse.

"Me too," I told her and followed Jared onto the sidewalk.

I was surprised to see his silver stuck still running and sitting in the middle of the road. I hesitated as he hurried around the front to the driver's side, bracing himself on the truck as he walked.

"Come on," he called out.

I carefully went to the passenger side and climbed into the warm cab. He put the truck in drive and eased it down the slope toward the road that led towards the mercantile.

"Jared, what's wrong?" I asked, my heart starting to beat wildly in my chest. The cab was silent. He never turned his radio off, which meant he had when he got in the truck. That wasn't like him at all, and neither was his serious expression or the tightness of his arms on the steering wheel.

"Marlee sent me an Instagram message," he said and paused.

"Why didn't she text me?" I asked and unzipped my purse. I pulled my phone out to find several missed calls and a few texts. Dad sent me two single texts to meet them at the hospital in Heritage City. Marlee asked several times where I was. Her final message was that Jared was coming. I felt like my heart was going to beat out of my chest and I couldn't manage to say a word, so I was glad when Jared answered my silent question.

"Margot was in an accident."

THE DRIVE to Heritage City was tense, quiet, and longer than normal. Jared drove slowly due to the weather. In the last hour, the snow started to come down heavier and the roads had several slick spots on the way down the mountain. When the weather was like this, we normally avoided going anywhere outside of Crescent City. I was glad that Jared was behind the wheel because a part of me was so nervous about Margot that I wanted to ask him to drive faster.

Once we were farther down the mountain, the roads weren't quite as slick, and Jared did pick up speed a bit. The snow was still thick, and traffic moved slowly.

"Why are there so many people out?" I groaned.

"The last of the grocery store rush, probably," Jared said as he stopped at a red light. "We weren't expected to get it this bad."

I hadn't checked the weather in days, and I was in such a witchy bubble that I wasn't worried about the roads with the lodge being dry thanks to the witches. I noticed that I was bouncing my legs now that we were forced to wait. The hospital was in downtown Heritage City, four more lights away.

"Have you heard from anyone?" Jared asked.

I shook my head as I checked my phone again. I'd tried calling Marlee and my parents on the drive down, but the signal was too spotty on the mountain and the weather was only adding to the problem. Even in town, I had fewer bars than normal and not a single text or returned call.

"I don't know what that means," I said, feeling my eyes burn. Were they trying to figure out how to deliver bad news?

"I'm sure they're just busy," Jared said as the light turned green, and the line of cars got a very delayed start again. "They may not know anything either. Margot's where she needs to be right now. They'll take care of her."

His reassurance felt warm, and it only made the tears spill over. I took a few deep breaths to calm myself and then used the sleeve of my shirt to dab at my eyes, the fabric coming away with mascara smears.

We hit every light on the way to the hospital and the wait was worse when we were close enough to see the lights for the hospital ahead. Jared kept his voice calm every time he spoke to me, reminding me that Margot was being cared for, that my family were already there for her, and all the right words.

"I've never been to a hospital before," I said.

Jared was quiet as he pulled into the hospital parking lot.

"There's a receptionist just inside the doors. I'll drop you off and—"

"Come with me. I don't think..." I started to feel the panic creep up again. I was already a worried mess about what I might be walking into, I didn't need to stumble around a hospital blind on top of that.

"Okay. Can do," Jared said and drove right on past the covered drop-off line for the parking lot. He had to drive past several rows before he spotted an empty parking place. He was just as quick as I was to step out of the truck.

We carefully walked toward the entrance, both of us nearly wiping out on the icy lot twice. Once we reached the sliding doors, Jared led the way to the main desk where we were greeted with a rush of warm air and the smile of a woman with braids to her waist.

"Visiting, appointment, or seeking care?" she asked.

"Visiting," Jared told her before he even reached the desk. The woman looked down from us and began typing away at her computer.

"Patient's name, please," she said.

"Margot Sinclair. She would've been admitted a few hours ago from a car accident up the mountain," Jared said.

My heart raced as fast as the woman typed. Once she found what she was looking for, she looked up again.

"It's family only for now," she said.

"I-I'm Madison Sinclair. I'm her sister," I managed to say. I fumbled for my purse and my wallet fell out. Jared was quick to pick it up and hold it out to me. I pulled out my driver's license and flashed it at the woman.

"Give me one moment to call the desk," she said and reached for the phone.

I turned from the desk and stuffed my ID back in my wallet. I tried to block out the sound of the woman on the phone, worried what details I might overhear. Jared stayed right by me, helping me put my wallet back into my purse.

How long had it been? When was Margot even admitted? I checked my texts again and call history. It took us almost two hours to get down here because of the weather. My parents and Marlee started to reach out an hour before Jared and I left.

"How did you find me?" I asked, more for the distraction than out of curiosity.

"Marlee told me you'd been reading somewhere in town," he said. "She said she wasn't sure where, but she thought maybe it was a place we'd gone together because she couldn't find you in town when she drove through. A pink Jeep is hard to miss, so I was surprised to see it sitting outside the café after I didn't find you at the lodge."

I bet they'd both just missed me. While I was asking Winnie to meet up to make amends, Margot was at the hospital and Marlee was launching a search party for me. It didn't hit me until now that his first thought was to check the lodge.

"Why did you go to the lodge?" I asked.

"I guess I thought that…" Jared let out a deep breath. "That's where everything changed. I guess I thought you would feel the same about that place as I do."

I could've argued that everything changed here in Heritage City.

"Madison," the woman called out. I turned around and walked right up to the desk again.

"What's going on?" I asked.

She looked back at me like she hadn't expected me to ask that. After a moment of hesitation, she said, "You can go up to floor two, dear."

"What about me?" Jared asked.

She gave him a sympathetic smile. "You can go with her, but you'll have to wait in the lounge."

"Okay. Thank you," Jared told her and led the way to the elevator behind the round desk.

I was glad he was handling all the details. He pressed the button for the second floor, and we waited with the soft Christmas jazz music playing the background on the way up. When the doors slid apart, he walked right out and up to another round desk where two nurses were stationed.

"Madison Sinclair?" one asked and then looked from me to Jared. "You'll have to wait through the door on the left."

I looked back at Jared as the nurse started down the hallway of doors.

"It'll be fine," he told me with a small smile.

I turned and followed the man halfway down the hall. He knocked on the wooden door and then opened it. I could hear the TV in the background playing music. A glance at the screen over the man's head told me it was a New Year's Eve concert. When the man moved to the bed, I saw Marlee sitting on a chair in the corner and my parents sitting together in a window seat.

"How are you feeling, Margot?" the nurse asked.

"Fine."

"Any pain?"

"Not anymore," she said.

Margot was in a hospital gown and sitting up in the large bed. She had a thick blue blanket draped over her legs and an IV taped to the back of her right hand. She looked up at me and forced a half-smile on her face, one that I hadn't seen since her club soccer team lost their final game of her senior season.

"If you need anything, just call," the man told her.

He left without another word and the only sound was the cheering of the crowd in Time's Square. I took a couple more steps into the room, looking over Margot for any serious signs of injury.

"Are you okay?" I asked.

Margot scoffed. "Physically."

"Skidded off the road and took a nosedive a way down the mountain," Dad said. "We're lucky the car didn't roll."

My skin went cold at the thought. I both wanted more details and never hoped to hear them.

"Are you okay?" I asked again.

Margot pushed the blankets down so I could see both of her legs. The hospital gown was hiked up high on her thighs and both legs were in casts past her knees. She didn't say a word but recovered her legs a moment after with a look of frustration.

"She broke both her legs in a few places. The right was worse than the left. The doctor said she might need surgery on her knee," Mom said.

I wanted to know how long the recovery would be, but it didn't matter. Margot would think it was too long.

"I'm glad it wasn't worse," I said and got a mutter of agreement from everyone in the room but Margot. She let out a long sigh and just nodded, looking up at the TV mounted on the far wall.

"They said they can wheel me out tomorrow," Margot said.

I let out a deep sigh and felt the tightness in my chest ease. I wrapped my arms around Margot's shoulders and then joined Marlee on the other side of the room, feeling exhausted.

Chapter 24

THE WEATHER EASED LATER that night, but Marlee and I decided to stay overnight with Margot, most of us. Mom and Dad went to the house to prepare to have Margot home for a while. She would have to stay downstairs, so they needed to come to terms with giving up some of their office space to make room for a bed unless they wanted her to sleep on the couch. Honestly, I half expected them to just set her up on the couch.

Marlee and I talked with Margot as much as she'd let us. She didn't say anything about it, but we knew she was super bummed out about the future of her soccer career. Dad was already talking about her taking the semester off and maybe returning to UCLA in the fall to continue classes. She insisted on moving her classes so she could take them all virtually, which I agreed to help her do so she didn't have to worry so much.

Like that would keep her from worrying.

"You reached out to Jared," I said after Margot had given up on talking and was focused on a rerun of *Sex and the City* on TV.

Marlee shrugged, running her finger along the edges of her paperback book.

"I figured he would know where to find you," she said. "Clearly, I was right."

"As always," I told her.

She smiled and said, "Not about *everything*."

"I'd like to hear about the things you get wrong, Marlee Mouse," I said, using an old nickname she'd hated when we were little. She didn't recoil like normal at hearing it. She chewed on her lower lip as if thinking hard.

"Part of me thought you were too..." She let out a sigh instead of finishing the insult I knew was coming. I was stuck-up. I was bitchy. "I thought you'd be over it by now."

I felt my stomach sink a bit as I thought about my own drama. Everything with Margot had me so nervous that I'd forgotten about Jared. I'd have to thank him for the ride at some point.

"I've never met someone who didn't see everything else about me, like our family name, the trips abroad, all that stuff," I said.

Marlee nodded and moved the book aside so she could rest her forearms on the table between us.

"I like him," she said, the words so firm that it was like she was trying to convey some other message. Maybe I really wasn't as smart as my youngest sister, because I needed her to spell it out.

"I know you all do," I said and motioned to Margot on the bed. She didn't even look our way. "I do too. I don't know that he can unsee the old version of me now. I don't know that he can separate who I am now from that person after everything."

"He came," Marlee said as if that was all I needed to know.

"Because he's a super nice guy," I said.

She groaned and after glancing at Margot, who was still staring at the TV like it had offended her in some way, she looked back at me with a serious expression.

"You said when we were dress shopping that things couldn't work with Jared because you were in different states, so on and so on," she said and rolled her eyes. "What I know is that relationships, any relationships, don't work unless you do. If you want to be with someone, really be with them, you figure out a way to make it work. If that doesn't line up, then maybe it wasn't meant to be. But you moping around all of Crescent City tells me you want this to work out."

"I don't know that it matters what I want," I said under my breath.

Marlee scoffed. "He found you."

She raised her eyebrows in that challenging way she always did when she made a good point. It was that very look that we all thought would make her a good lawyer, that unspoken cue that she knew the truth without needing to hear it.

"I think I'm going to get something to drink. Want anything?" I asked after a long moment. I stood up and Marlee shook her head. She moved her book closer to her and opened it to her bookmark.

"Margot, do you want anything?" I asked.

"No. I'm fine," she said without looking my way.

I left the room and walked toward the main desk. I was sure there was a vending machine in the lounge, but I didn't expect to see Jared there.

"What are you still doing here?" I asked.

He was lying across a couch next to the vending machine with a similar blue blanket to the one draped over Margot in her room. He'd balled up his coat to use as a pillow. He sat up and cleared his throat, his hair sticking up on one side as if he'd been asleep there for a while. I checked the clock on the wall. It was four in the morning, and he was still here.

"I stayed in case you needed anything," he said. "I wanted to make sure everything was okay. How's Margot?"

I moved into the room and sat at the end of the couch. He gathered the blanket in a pile and stuck it behind him to make space.

"She's all right. She broke both of her legs, and they think she may need a knee surgery down the road, but it depends on how she heals. She'll be here in Heritage City at least this semester," I said.

He nodded slowly. "That's good."

I nodded. My index finger ran over the zipper of my purse. I heard the nurses at the main desk talking, one of them bursting into loud laughter at something the other said. The vending machine hummed next to us. I hadn't really come for anything to drink. Mostly, I wanted to walk. I figured I'd come back with a can or bottle of something and just let it sit on the table until someone asked to have it.

"You found me," I said, repeating the words Marlee used before I'd left.

"You needed me," Jared replied and looked back at me with the sincerest gaze that nearly made my chest burst.

"I decided to change my major to business," I said.

Jared smiled and said, "I think you'll be good at that."

Silence stretched between us. I was just about to tell him that I was thinking about moving back home to go to school in Denver when he spoke.

"Winnie told me you two had a lot to talk about," he said and turned his phone between his hands. "She told me why she broke up with me and how things wouldn't have worked out and I agreed. I don't know why I ever thought… I think I was just fitting the mold of every other business study in my classes."

"I think I've been doing that too," I said. "I like fashion, but I never really saw myself outfitting a runway model and I defi-nitely don't want to live in New York or anywhere bigger than Heritage City. I don't want to make those kinds of clothes or run that kind of big business."

Jared snorted. I was surprised to see that boyish smile on his face that I loved so much. He sucked in a deep breath and sat up, setting his phone aside and turning to face me.

"I wanted to forget about everything and just move on. Classes start next week; I'm going back to Denver. I really wanted everything to just be summed up as some Christmas Break fling, but I kept looking at our pictures and looking through your Instagram. Sounds a little creepy to say it aloud," he said with a laugh.

"No, I-we had a good time. I have been having a hard time accepting that it was…" I couldn't bring myself to say it was a fling, because it didn't feel that way at all. It felt like it had been months. I felt like I knew him deeper than anyone I'd met this year.

"I found your website," he said.

My heart skipped. My website was public. I had all my products listed as unavailable since I started working on it. I figured having it public, even if I wasn't ready to officially launch, would at least build a bit of interest in my future brand.

"It's a work in progress," I said and laughed. "It's pretty rough."

"The mission statement is there," Jared said and shifted closer to me. "That's all I needed to know."

There was a split moment of hesitation before he leaned in and kissed me. I moved closer to him, glad that no one was in the room to witness the way I pressed his back against the vending machine. The kiss lasted so long that it was almost embarrassing considering where we were and when I pulled back, I glanced at the doorway to make sure we didn't have any spectators.

Jared smiled back at me.

"I think this vending machine has bottled water," he said with a laugh.

I slapped my hand playfully against his chest.

"Better buy two," he joked.

JARED STAYED LONG ENOUGH to talk with my family and help us transition from the tiny hospital room down to the hospital entrance where we decided who was riding in what car. Mom, Dad, Marlee, and Margot went in the SUV along with the new wheelchair Margot would need as she healed. I rode with Jared in his truck, and we stopped to pick up breakfast for everyone on the way.

Margot seemed to perk up a bit once we got home. I think some of that was being away from the doctors and nurses and all the worry over her legs but having Jared around to toss a joke into the mix every now and then was one perk of having him around. We ate gathered around the living room with an episode of *The Office* in the background. Mostly, Jared and Dad talked over it about the Denver Broncos.

"I told you," Marlee whispered to me when I joined her in the kitchen for a second helping of breakfast tacos.

"I know," I said. "Marlee Sinclair is always right."

She gave a satisfied smirk before retreating to the living room with her plate. I ate at the kitchen counter, watching my dad argue with Jared about the coaches who recently left. The debate was getting heated until Jared made some joke my brain didn't understand. Whatever it was, my dad thought it was hilarious and laughed in a way I hadn't heard in a very long time. It actually gained everyone's attention and to my mom's annoyance, he insisted she wouldn't understand.

Jared, Marlee, and I drove back to Crescent City in the truck. Margot's Jeep had been totaled in the accident, but mine was still sitting outside the café and we had to clean up the cabin for the season. Jared dropped me off to take the Jeep and I followed his truck up the mountain.

The cabin was worse than I thought. Apparently, Dad was in the middle of making salmon before they left and the entire downstairs reeked so bad of old fish that I almost gagged.

"I'll take care of the kitchen," Jared told us and followed the stench. "You two can gather all the clothes and things."

Marlee and I started with our own rooms. She was done so quickly that she was on to Margot's room before I had even finished moving my clothes from the closet. I finished zipping my pink suitcase and took it downstairs, setting it next to Marlee's and Margot's. Then I prepared myself to join Jared in the kitchen.

Marlee could manage Mom and Dad's stuff on her own, right?

Despite the dishwasher to his left, Jared insisted on washing all the dirty dishes and was working now to dry them off and replace them in the cabinets. I helped. We worked in silence for a long time with only the sound of some podcast on his phone in the background.

"Long distance," I said. Even the word made me sad. Ugh.

"Yup," he answered and put the last cup up and turned to face me. He picked up his phone and paused the podcast. "It won't be so bad. Remember what I said about texting and Face-Time?" He winked.

"Maybe I should just transfer," I said.

We talked about this. We'd done more than that. We looked up all the information at both schools to see what the process entailed, and it was too late to get everything for the semester. I'd have to settle for the business classes I'd switched to at Kent and see how things went.

"It will be fine," Jared said and kissed my forehead.

Marlee came down with Mom and Dad's suitcases, doing an awkward waddle to set them down with ours by the door. Jared and I helped load the Jeep and then we had to part ways. We kissed long enough in the garage that Marlee leaned over and honked the Jeep's horn, startling us both apart.

"I'll pick you up early," Jared told me as he fished his keys out of his pocket. "I'll drop you off at the airport on my way back to campus."

I dreaded it.

Marlee and I drove back to Heritage City and actually talked the entire way. I wanted to know what she really thought about *Christmas as We Know It* and she unleashed her typical analysis of the book from the plot to the characters. She talked so much about it that I wasn't sure if she liked it until she told me she had at the end.

I waited until the night before I left to repack all the things I'd take back to Ohio. I didn't sleep well and was up earlier than I needed to be. When Jared got to the house, my whole family was up and ready to say their goodbyes. Margot was a little sad not to be going to the airport with me as we planned, but she told me she was ready to sit through Professor Klein's lectures from the living room couch in her pajamas.

We loaded my suitcase into the backseat of the truck, and we left Heritage City for Denver, Jared initiating a karaoke session on the way there. I kept all my emotions at bay while he parked, and rolled my suitcase inside. He followed me as far as he could, and we said goodbye. We kissed shamelessly in the middle of the walkway, and I promised I'd call once my flight landed. He promised me everything would be fine and that I'd love my business classes and would wonder why I hadn't switched sooner.

I cried on the plane.

Chapter 25

I WAS SO mad when our flight was delayed. Pissed.

Once we took off, I relaxed a little. The girl next to me was close to my age, her name was Jazzlyn Mark, and was flying to Denver for the summer to go on a camping trip with her family. She was super nice and bought me a rum and coke when she heard my twenty-first birthday was a few weeks ago.

We walked together through the busy airport, talking about everything we wanted to do this summer.

"My mom and I always hike while my dad and brother go fishing," she said as we made our way to the baggage claim. "I think this year we are doing Gray's Peak and Torrey's Peak."

"My boyfriend and I are hiking Gray's this summer," I said, worrying a moment after that I might've come off a little too excited. She didn't seem to notice. She was just as excited about her outdoorsy vacation plans.

"When? Maybe we can link up," she said.

"I'm not sure yet, but I can reach out when I know," I said.

"If you can, you should plan it around the end of June. We'll be in the area for a week or two. We could go out."

I pulled my phone from my purse as she did the same. We exchanged numbers while we waited for our flight's luggage to appear on the carousel. Once we grabbed our things, me with both giant suitcases in hand and my backpack on both shoulders, we made our way toward the front of the airport.

"I'll see you another time," Jazzlyn said and gave me a wave before she started toward the far exit. I waved back and promised to reach out after I'd talked with Jared about our hike.

I didn't have to walk very far before I found him. I felt my throat closing and my eyes burned. He looked handsome as ever. I was so used to seeing him in sweaters and coats that it was a little weird to see him in a pair of jeans and a gray long-sleeve shirt. He held a single balloon that had Elsa from *Frozen's* face on both sides.

I let go of my bags to run to him and wrap my arms around his neck. We kissed before he reminded me about my luggage several feet away.

"You know what they say about leaving your bags unattended," he laughed. He went to retrieve them, rolling them out of the airport and to the parking lot as I told him about how my flight was and meeting Jazzlyn.

"We can probably go in June," he said. "Ask her exactly when they're hiking Gray's."

"I will. She was really nice." I got into the truck and opened Instagram to see if I could find her profile. Thankfully, it didn't take long, and her profile picture looked just like her.

"Did you get the results from all your finals?" Jared asked as he backed out of the parking spot.

I let out a dramatic gasp that made him laugh.

"I made an A on Intro to Economics class. I was worried about that one," I said. I knew a lot of math was involved in business, but I hadn't taken a math class since freshman year and was worried about all the formulas.

"Damn. I think I made a B in mine," he said. "Maybe Colorado's just harder."

I elbowed him as he moved toward the highway. He laughed and turned the radio on to his usual station. I'd missed it. Sometimes, when I was too busy to call him as often as I'd like to, I'd listen to that station when I got ready for bed. Rainy hated it. After this semester, she was the only thing I'd miss about Kent State. We'd become good friends and I promised her I'd keep in touch.

"Did that link for Marlee's graduation livestream work? Her speech was great," Jared said.

"It worked. I still can't download all your pictures. I don't know why," I told him and opened the photo app on my phone. I assumed it was my signal and then I wondered if the files were just too large. I knew I could always get them later or just see them on Marlee's Instagram. She posted just about all of them plus two different photos of her posing with her valedictorian trophy. It was her profile picture now.

Jared gave me the updates about his mom and uncle as we drove. Not a lot was new except that the farm was booming compared to this time last year. With my help, they expanded the shop and added quite a bit more clothing to the mix. We found a few other small businesses' who let the McAdams carry some of their products in the shop like more candles and some amazing bath bombs from a lady in Telluride.

We stopped talking when we reached a nice apartment complex not far from the University of Colorado's campus. Jared typed in the gate code and continued through the streets. He parked the truck under a carpark and started to unload my luggage as I got out.

"Third floor, right?" I asked.

Jared joined me at the back of the truck with both my suit-cases in hand and wearing my pink backpack.

"Yeah. Sorry about the climb," he said.

"We'll call it training for all those fourteeners," I said.

He laughed as we went to the stairs, telling me I'd need a lot more cardio than that to get in shape for some of those hikes. I went all the way to the top and then let him lead the way to the end of the landing where a red door was with a welcome mat on the concrete. He unlocked the door and went inside. I followed him and felt the excitement bubble over.

It wasn't huge. It was a one-bedroom, one-bath apartment with a combination living room and kitchen. I was just glad we had our own washer and dryer, and I didn't have to lug my underwear to some communal center. The living room was exactly the way I'd seen it on FaceTime and Zoom calls with the gray couch and armchair and the oak table. Another door next to the TV led to the bedroom. A door next to the kitchen opened to the bathroom, which was thankfully larger than I worried it would be with a combination shower/tub and a large countertop that I knew I'd soon cover with all my makeup and hair products.

I went into the bedroom. Jared's bed was covered in gray sheets the same shade as the living room furniture. The bedroom was just large enough for a small desk under the window. I took off my purse and set it on the window and looked out over the parking lot. You could see the tops of a few of the college buildings from here.

I turned from the window to find Jared leaning against the doorway with a smile on his face.

"Welcome home," he said. "Is it possible for a winter witch to look forward to a sunny Colorado summer?"

I put my arms around his waist and rose onto my toes. "It'll be a first for me," I said and kissed him.

ACKNOWLEDGMENTS

This book came to me just before the holidays right after I published *Guardians of the Sixth Gate* and needed a break from the seriousness of the series. I plotted out the book on my phone overnight and started writing it the next day. The entire process was a whirlwind that completely swept me away and led me on an adventure that was completely new to me. I'm not new to writing romance, but I had never written a book where the main plot was the romance, and the fantasy was the subplot. I learned a lot along the way and fell in love with a new angle of writing I'd never thought I would ever attempt.

Thanks to my sister, Abby, for inspiring aspects of Madison Sinclair's character. Growing up with you was always eventful and there was never a dull moment with you around, and still isn't. Thank you to Katie Steier for your support through my publishing journey and for never being afraid to tell me when something sucks. I love and appreciate our friendship. And as always, thank you Lucia for all your hard work helping me edit this book. No matter how polished I think each manuscript is, you manage to find ways to make it better and I thank you for your eye for detail.

ABOUT THE AUTHOR

Amy Prokopis is a fiction author from Oklahoma who writes fantasy books. She loves writing everything from science fiction and fantasy to contemporary romance. She graduated from Oklahoma State University with a bachelor's degree in English and a minor in German before obtaining a master's degree in school counseling. Besides writing, Amy enjoys distance running and spending time with her husband, their son, and their Havanese, June.

ALSO BY AMY PROKOPIS

TURN THE PAGE FOR A SNEAK PEEK
OF CURSE OF WINGS AND DARKNESS

CHAPTER 1

"Our final is same time next week," Dr. Bartlett said as everyone finished gathering their things in the lecture hall. "Don't forget to buy a blue book from the student store for the essay portion."

I zipped up my backpack, holding my water bottle between both of my hands as I waited for the rest of my row to file toward the exit ahead of me. I let out a deep breath, then another, then another. The longer I waited, the more I worried that I would be stuck in the lecture hall with our professor who'd told me last week that my essay was trash. I stuffed the paper in my notebook before I had even gotten to the end of it, it was that bad. I was having nightmares that ended with red letters, making it hard to even make the walk here for class without feeling like my heart was going to burst from my chest.

I caught Dr. Bartlett's eye, quickly averting my gaze and squeezing past the last two girls at the end of the row.

"Sorry. I need to... I have a thing," I said as I nearly tripped over their feet to get to the aisle. I hurried up the last of the steps and out the back door. Four steps exactly and I was outside the building and in the fresh air, the cool air making my lungs contract when I breathed it in. Still, it was better than being in that tight lecture hall.

It wasn't until my heart slowed that I realized I'd been walking the opposite direction and I turned to make my way north toward the apartment. Thank God this was my last class of the week. Pre-finals week was hell. You'd think it would get easier by your third semester, but I was a nervous wreck the entire week the same way I was freshman year.

When I turned around, I noticed a boy leaning against the wall of the building. He was hot, with curly blonde hair and blue eyes that I thought pierced my soul even from six feet away. He straightened up and smiled.

"Hey," he said. "You have a class in there, right? I've seen you get out at eight every Monday, Wednesday, and Friday."

I nodded, a weird sound of approval coming out.

"Damn. I didn't mean it like… I'm not, like, watching you or anything. I have a class in this building that gets out at the same time," he said and gestured toward the building he'd been leaning against before. "Are you a film, English, drama…"

"Music," I said and cleared my throat. "I'm a music major, cello."

He nodded as though considering what the words meant.

"Very cool. What's your name?" he asked.

"Um, Lily," I said, my heart starting to pick up pace again.

"Good to meet you," he said and extended his hand. When I took it to give it a shake, he stepped forward, close enough now that I could smell him. I couldn't place the smell, but it was the best thing I'd smelled in a long time. It was like the best pastry, comforting.

"G-good to meet you too," I said and backed away, placing my hand on my water bottle and turning it between my hands.

"I'll see you around," he said. "Maybe next week, hopefully sooner."

The way he said it paired with the way his eyes roved over me before he turned and left had me a blushing mess. I was a puddle. I melted right there and anyone and everyone could probably see that I was having a nervous breakdown over a boy I didn't know. Even now that he was halfway across the court-yard, I was struggling to calm myself. I didn't even know his name. What was wrong with me? Why didn't I think to ask his name?

I walked in the direction of our apartment, walking faster than I had planned just to try to match the rhythm of my heart. Exercise was good for anxiety. I knew that from therapy. Exercise always helped me to get a grip and clear my head. So, I walked fast until I was at the front entrance to our apartment. I scanned my card and walked into the lobby, walking right past the front desk like normal, and went to the elevator.

Our apartment was at the top, so I had while in the elevator to decompress. I felt tears well in my eyes before I slowed my breathing, using a technique I'd learned from my Intro to Psychology class. When the elevator dinged and the door slid open, I walked much calmer down the hall. Our apartment was at the end of the hall, the last room. It meant that my bedroom had a window that looked over the street and the city lights.

I turned my key in the lock and walked in, finding Anne at the stove making dinner like she normally did.

"Hey," she said and tucked a loose strand of dark hair behind her ear. "How was class?"

"Good," I said and passed her for my bedroom.

Just past the tiny kitchen was a shared living room with a wall of windows that opened onto the balcony. To the left was Anne's room and to the right was mine. Hers had strings of blue Christmas lights hanging around the perimeter and mine had a magenta color. I went to my room and sat my backpack on the desk chair, stepping out of my tennis shoes and tossing my socks toward the hamper where one bounced off the plastic and settled on the hardwood floor.

"I have ramen ready," Anne called.

It was a Friday tradition. Anne made ramen and I came home from class to eat it with her. Each week was a different kind of ramen, but it was always ramen. Most nights, we would go out in the city. Her favorite spot was a club just down the street that was frequented by other NYU students.

We ate in silence for a long time. I finished most of my dish, only some of the warm broth left before we moved to the living room to watch TV. Anne pulled up an old episode of Ru Paul's Drag Race, one of our favorite seasons. I sipped the broth from the bowl as she finished her helping and set it aside, eager to make conversation judging by the way she sat forward on the couch.

"We should go to the club tonight," she said.

I knew that what she really meant was that we should go out and find people to hook up with. I was still figuring out how to navigate that arena. It wasn't like I was a novice or anything. I'd had sex. It was horrible, but I did it. I just shook it off and told myself that everyone's first time was terrible. Still, though, did it really count if you laid there because you didn't know what to do and the guy figured out after a few thrusts that you were a virgin? Did it really count if he changed his mind halfway in and left?